Rosa

Law &
Beard

Book 8 of The Dixie Warden Rejects

By

Lani Lynn Vale

ISBN-13:
978-1985648210

ISBN-10:
1985648210

Dedication

Dedications blow big balls when you've already dedicated a book to everyone you like (all eighty of them). (Just kidding) (Kind of).

Anyway, I'm going to write about something I think is awesome. Naps. I bet you don't take enough naps, and you are really doing yourself a disservice by not taking them. I take one every day if I can. Sometimes all I can fit in is thirty minutes. Other times, it's a full blown four-hour nap.

Napping makes me a better person. It also helps me write better so I'm not sitting here typing useless shit to reread later and think, WTF did I just write?

Anyway, if this is coherent, you can thank my nap.

Acknowledgements

Joe Adams- Model

Golden Czermak- Photographer

Danielle Palumbo- My awesome content editor.

Ellie McLove & Ink It Out Editing- My editors

My mom- Thank you for reading this book eight million two hundred times.

Cheryl, Leah, Kathy, Mindy, Barbara & Amanda—I don't know what I would do without y'all. Thank you, my lovely betas, for loving my books as much as I do.

CONTENTS

Prologue- Page 11
Chapter 1- Page 15
Chapter 2- Page 19
Chapter 3- Page 29
Chapter 4- Page 39
Chapter 5- Page55
Chapter 6- Page 75
Chapter 7- Page 83
Chapter 8- Page 91
Chapter 9- Page 99
Chapter 10- Page 119
Chapter 11- Page 147
Chapter 12- Page 157
Chapter 13- Page 165
Chapter 14- Page 177
Chapter 15- Page 189
Chapter 16- Page 201
Chapter 17- Page 219
Chapter 18- Page 229
Chapter 19- Page 245
Chapter 20- Page 251
Chapter 21- Page 263
Chapter 22- Page 267
Epilogue- Page 277

Other titles by Lani Lynn Vale:

The Freebirds
Boomtown

Highway Don't Care

Another One Bites the Dust

Last Day of My Life

Texas Tornado

I Don't Dance

The Heroes of The Dixie Wardens MC
Lights To My Siren

Halligan To My Axe

Kevlar To My Vest

Keys To My Cuffs

Life To My Flight

Charge To My Line

Counter To My Intelligence

Right To My Wrong

Code 11- KPD SWAT
Center Mass

Double Tap

Bang Switch

Execution Style

Charlie Foxtrot

Kill Shot

Coup De Grace

The Uncertain Saints

Lani Lynn Vale

Whiskey Neat

Jack & Coke

Vodka On The Rocks

Bad Apple

Dirty Mother

Rusty Nail

The Kilgore Fire Series

Shock Advised

Flash Point

Oxygen Deprived

Controlled Burn

Put Out

I Like Big Dragons Series

I Like Big Dragons and I Cannot Lie

Dragons Need Love, Too

Oh, My Dragon

The Dixie Warden Rejects

Beard Mode

Fear the Beard

Son of a Beard

I'm Only Here for the Beard

The Beard Made Me Do It

Beard Up

For the Love of Beard

Law & Beard

There's No Crying in Baseball

Pitch Please

Furious George (Spring 2018)

The Hail Raisers
Hail No

Go to Hail

Burn in Hail

What the Hail

The Hail You Say

Hail Mary

The Simple Man Series

Kinda Don't Care (4-5-18)

Maybe Don't Wanna (5-4-18)

Get You Some (6-7-18)

PROLOGUE

*To everyone that received a book from me for Christmas, they're
due back at the library by Friday.*
-How you know you're poor

Winnie

Conleigh slammed the door shut, and she locked it for good
measure.

I sighed and looked out the window, hoping to find the patience to
move on from this new teenage attitude that my recently minted
sixteen-year-old was throwing at me.

My eyes caught on our new neighbor, and I gasped.

My new neighbor was gorgeous.

He was wearing a tight pair of Wrangler jeans that fit him like a
glove, a black faded t-shirt, and a belt that held a big black gun to
his hip. Next to the big black gun was a gold shield, one that I
couldn't read from this distance, but I knew to be a shield for the
Mooresville, AL Police Department.

"You going to do okay there?"

I smiled and answered into my phone. "Yes," I sighed. "I'm going
to be okay here."

"Good, I'm glad." She sighed. "I'm home and trying to sort
through the mountain of expensive shit that my parents left me in

the will. Do you think they'd turn over in their graves if I burned the whole place down to the ground?"

"I'm pretty sure with that corrupt little police town you're living in, they'll find a way to charge you for it, then put you away for murder on top of that."

Krisney started to laugh.

"They're not that bad."

"No, they're not," I admitted. "How about you just go through the junk, hold an estate sale, and post a dollar on everything?"

Krisney started to giggle, but my attention was laser focused on the man who was no longer standing at his mailbox.

"Your neighbor," I found myself saying. "Who is he?"

"The one to the left, or the one across the street?" she questioned.

"Across the street. The silver-haired hottie who has muscles on top of muscles."

"Steel Cross, better known as Big Papa to his MC, or BP to the guys at the police department where he works," she answered instantly. "He was also one of the reasons I bought that house. I figured what better and safer neighborhood to buy into than one next to the chief of police."

"The chief of police?" I breathed. "You're shitting me."

"Nope," Krisney said. "Anyway, I gotta go. But he's really nice. Don't be scared to talk to him."

She hung up before I had a chance to say that there was never going to be a day that I'd talk to him. Not willingly. He was too pretty for me and my broken self. He'd probably chew me up and spit me out.

But as I watched him in all of his alpha male glory as he stepped in front of a speeding car, and then proceeded to give the teenager the lecture to end all lectures, I realized that if he ever spoke to me first, I'd have no choice but to talk to him.

The sheer magnetism of him was enthralling.

Lani Lynn Vale

CHAPTER 1

I'm at that age where a twenty-two-year-old is looking good…but so is his dad.
-Winnie's secret thoughts

Winnie

"Cody, no," I called, seeing my son, who was all of five years old, staring at me with the most heart-breaking expression on his face.

"Cody."

That came from Conleigh, my eldest daughter. Conleigh was sixteen, going on forty-three.

She was my surprise baby when I was sixteen. She was also more of a mom than I was at times—at least lately.

No, before you ask, they do not have the same father. Yes, my husband had loved Conleigh like she was his own, or at least, he had while we were married. Now, I wasn't so sure. Conleigh wasn't taking this move well. My husband had left me for another woman, and he then forced us to move out of our home because, technically, it all had been his when we'd gotten married.

"Mom, seriously?"

I looked up to see her staring at me with anger in her eyes.

"Seriously, what?" I growled. "I can't. I don't have any money, and I can't buy it for him right now."

"I do," she replied stubbornly.

I ground my teeth

"I know you do," I said. "But, unfortunately, he can't always get what he wants, and you need that money for lunch this week."

"I can make a lunch," she offered.

I looked up at the ceiling and counted to ten.

"He does not need the car. He has fifteen just like it at home. You do not need to buy it because you *have* to pay for lunch next week. Do not make me repeat it again."

Plus, Conleigh rarely ever got up in time to get herself out the door on a normal day. Adding making a lunch to the routine would surely make her later than she normally was.

We'd just pulled into the check-out lane when the sliding doors of the grocery store opened and two cops rolled in. One of them was my ex-husband, and the other was a man that looked downright appetizing.

Not that my ex-husband didn't look appetizing. He did.

He'd always been attractive.

But the man standing beside him? Yeah, he was gorgeous.

Then again, anything would look good next to my ex at this point.

My ex who had left me when I'd needed him the most.

"Daddy!"

I groaned as I watched my son run toward his father, who scooped him up and acted like he'd seen him only hours ago instead of the three months it had stretched out to.

I gritted my teeth and handed the lady my card.

"I'm sorry, but it's saying declined."

I gritted my teeth, then looked at the pint of ice cream that I'd thought to get as a reward for my day.

"Put that back," I murmured. "Oh, and this."

I handed over my baby wipes. I could use the rags that I'd been using over the last week. It seemed to be working all right.

She did as instructed, looking at me with pity in her eyes, and I ignored it.

"Okay, it went through."

I breathed a sigh of relief and started stacking my bags into the cart, pushing it stiffly out into the main aisle that would lead out of the store.

"Hello," I murmured to the officer who was with my ex.

"Hi." He smiled.

The smile didn't meet his eyes.

I was sure he was wondering, just like everyone else, why I'd 'left my husband.'

I hadn't. He'd left me.

But no one knew that because he told them something totally different than what actually happened.

And, since this town was so fucking small, and it'd been the town I'd been transplanted into when I'd married my ex, I didn't figure they'd believe me anyway.

My ex was a cop, the town heartthrob when he was growing up, and an all-around American hero.

An American hero to everyone but me.

"Let's go," I ordered softly to my daughter.

Conleigh walked over to her brother who was talking animatedly with his father and took him out of Matt's arms. Then she placed him on his feet and led him out without a word to my ex.

Cody went, but he only had eyes for his daddy as he walked grudgingly out of the store.

I didn't stop and talk to either of them as I passed, but I felt my ex's eyes on me the entire way.

Then again, I also felt like someone else was looking, too.

I pretended it was the other cop.

At least in dreams, I could still attract a man with the fucked-up body of mine.

CHAPTER 2

I've had my patience tested. I'm negative.
-Steel's secret thoughts

Steel

"Big Papa, seriously." Aaron growled. "This isn't going to work."

I rolled my eyes and walked away, leaving him to argue with himself.

He'd already given me his best argument, and I wasn't listening to the rest of the shit excuses he gave me.

I did not, under any circumstances, want to deal with that woman's shit today. So yes, I was ignoring her phone calls. I was also avoiding her.

But she was seriously fucking annoying, and I couldn't deal.

My phone rang, and I glanced at the screen, breathing a sigh of relief when I saw my son's name pop up instead of my ex's.

"Hey, boy," I said.

"Hey, Dad," Sean greeted. "Did you know that your ex is now calling *my* phone?"

I growled under my breath. "How does she even have your phone number?"

I knew for certain *I* hadn't given it to her.

"Don't know. But she calls and wakes up the baby again, I might very well have to contain my wife."

I chuckled under my breath, my eyes automatically scanning the gas station around me as I backed into a corner to take the call.

My eyes lit on a young girl, maybe sixteen or seventeen, who was browsing the aisle of crap that every gas station had. Earphones, air fresheners, tiny travel packs of Tylenol and ibuprofen. Things of that nature that you might need on a road trip.

Though, this one also had a little bit more than most since the station was one of those super ones that the truckers all used right off the interstate.

"I'm sorry, Sean. I don't know why Lizzibeth is calling. I've already spoken with her today and told her to stop calling everyone. I'll take her call again tonight when I'm off shift and figure it out. In the meantime, just keep doing what you're doing."

Sean grunted. "I will."

Then he hung up.

I shoved the phone into my pocket, continuing to keep my eyes on the girl.

Where I was, partially covered by a stack of Bud Light, meant that only my eyes and the top of my head were visible. Which had to be the reason why the girl, when she glanced around, didn't see me. Otherwise, I knew that she wouldn't have shoved two pairs of earphones into her jacket and then started to walk out the door.

I sighed and followed her out, gesturing to Aaron that I'd be outside.

He nodded his head and continued perusing the hotdogs rolling on the warmer.

"Hey, kid."

She looked up, startled to see me, and then her face fell.

She looked familiar, but I couldn't quite place her. It'd come back to me once she told me her name. I knew it.

"Let me have them." I gestured with my hand.

She looked down, then she pulled the earbuds out of the pocket of her jacket and placed them in the palm of my hand.

"Why did you steal these?"

She grimaced. "Because I needed them."

"You needed them so bad that you had to steal them?"

She looked away.

I knew she wasn't going to tell me why. Most of these teenagers didn't have a single bone in their body that gave them even a little bit of self-preservation.

"What's your name?"

She didn't hesitate to answer. "Conleigh."

The name didn't sound familiar, which surprised me. I knew nearly everyone in this town.

"Where do you live?"

"Off Mimosa."

My street.

"Let's go," I said to the girl.

"But my ride…"

"Your car can stay here until I speak with your parents."

The girl didn't say anything as I escorted her to my cruiser.

I could tell that she was worried.

She should be.

A police officer had just caught her stealing shit from a gas station.

But, if she hadn't truly looked terrified and repentant for stealing the earphones, then I would've booked her just because I could. Kids these days were getting worse and worse, and I wanted to make sure that she got herself straight now rather than being forced to do it the hard way later.

After depositing her in my cruiser, I went back inside and put the earphones on the counter.

"Let me get these."

"That all?" Patty, who was behind the counter today, asked.

I nodded.

She rang them up and said, "Seven dollars."

I handed her a ten, got my change, then gestured to Aaron who was still in front of the hot dogs. "Just get the boudin."

Then I left, leaving him to his own devices—and meat selection.

Once in my car, I made my way to my street—also her street—and asked for more specific information.

She directed me to the house that was directly across from mine.

Shit.

I knew who lived there.

I hadn't seen her—or her kids apparently—much, but I knew.

Winnifred Holyfield, Matt Holyfield's ex-wife. Matt Holyfield, a cop in my station. *Fuck.*

This kid's dad was a fucking cop. One of *my* fucking cops.

Goddammit.

I pulled into her driveway without another word, then got out.

Once I opened her door, I walked with her up to the front door and knocked before she could walk straight in.

There was some shuffling, and then the door opened.

Winnifred's eyes went to me, then to her daughter, and then back.

While she was busy checking me out, I was busy trying to remember how to breathe. Goddamn, but she was beautiful. She could've passed for the troublemaker's big sister, even though I knew she was her mom.

Her face fell in the interim.

"Conleigh," she whispered.

That's when Conleigh broke down.

"I just wanted some headphones that I didn't have to share with all the other poor kids." She burst out into explosive sobs. "Everyone makes fun of me!"

Winnifred's eyes closed, and her own tears started to fall.

And that was when I realized that there was much more to this situation than met the eye.

"Come in," she pulled the door open wide, and then stepped back.

My eyes went to the walker that was helping Winnifred walk, and I was suddenly very confused.

Last week, she hadn't been using a walker. Hell, she hadn't looked anything but in control of her faculties.

But she had been leaning quite heavily on that shopping cart, I told myself.

She'd also glared rather glacially at her ex-husband like he was the worst of scum.

Which had me confused, too.

Matt had told everyone *she'd* left *him*. I'd only assumed that it was due to something in their relationship, but now I had a whole lot of questions running through my mind.

The most important of which being: *Who left who?*

Because this woman in front of me didn't look like she would leave her husband. Not with a young kid who looked to be about four or five and a sixteen-year-old. Not when she couldn't afford to make it on her own…which reminded me of a promise that I'd made to a friend a couple of months back.

Her name was Krisney, and she'd bought this house.

After moving back home following her parents' deaths, she'd asked me to help keep an eye on it.

I had…peripherally.

Now I wondered if it wasn't the house that I was supposed to keep an eye on, but its occupants.

"Conleigh, head to your room, please," Winnifred said tiredly.

I waited until she was down the hall with the door closed before I turned my eyes to the mother.

"Thank you for bringing her home," she whispered. "I'm so sorry."

I studied the tired woman. "What's going on that she can't afford headphones?"

Then I placed the headphones on the table with the receipt.

Winnifred swallowed.

Why really wasn't any of my business, but when a teenage kid—one belonging to a cop at that—made the decision to steal, I kinda wanted to know why.

And she wasn't an exception.

Technically, she didn't have to tell me anything. Then again, I could've just as easily taken the kid to jail rather than to her mother's.

"Winnifred…"

"Winnie," she corrected, then sighed. "As for why, well…that's a long story."

"I'm more than up to hearing it."

And I was, too. I really, really wanted to know, although I really wasn't sure why the hell that was.

Winnie looked down at her hands and then sighed. "I don't have time. I have to be at work in a few minutes." She looked torn. "And…" she shook her head, looking sick to her stomach. "I'm sorry."

The tears in her eyes were what convinced me to let her go and not push her, so I did.

I tipped my hat—a simple black ball cap that said 'MPD' on it—and turned to walk away.

I did notice, however, that she watched me go the entire way.

I walked down the badly-in-need-of-a-mow front lawn, and straight to my cruiser in the driveway, not once turning around. I was damn proud of myself.

It was soft, sweet women like her, with their hearts in their eyes, that were the most trouble. I, too, had a soft spot…one that was hell when you were also a cop. One that had always been there, and always would be there, thanks to one particular girl—one just like the trouble-making Conleigh—whom I'd met during one of my first weeks on the job. One who was, I thought, just a pain in the ass. One who, weeks after I tried to set her straight, was killed by her father because I had brought her home drunk.

Shaking off my morose thoughts, I opened the door to my cruiser and got in.

Once I was settled, I called Fender.

"Yo," he answered.

"You know the neighbor across the street from me?"

"The one with the two kids?"

"Yeah," I confirmed. "Those."

"A little, why?"

"Her husband—ex-husband—is Matt Holyfield from work. Do you know what happened to her? The last time I saw her, she was running fucking marathons."

And she had been. Winnie Holyfield had been a goddamn record breaker. She ran marathons all over the world before she'd gotten married to Matt. It'd been a big deal when she'd lined up for a ten-kilometer race in a benefit for the president of our motorcycle club, the Dixie Wardens, better known as the Dixie Warden Rejects.

Stone had died unexpectedly, and to help cover funeral expenses for his wife, the town had held a ten-kilometer race. Winnie Holyfield had shown up, and she hadn't been alone. She'd brought a ton of her friends. Her tons of friends who had told their tons of friends, and then suddenly, our little ten-kilometer race had turned into a fucking benefit the size of which I'd never seen.

The ten-kilometer race had turned into a half-marathon from there, and it'd gotten a ton of media coverage. And when I say a ton, I mean a fucking *ton*. The race had more than covered funeral expenses for our president. His wife, Mei, hadn't had to shell out a single dime.

Not that she was going to anyway.

I had planned to pay for it. All of it.

But I hadn't needed to thanks to *her*.

Winnie.

Fender made a sound in his throat, and then clicked with his teeth.

"I think she had a spinal stroke," he said. "I remember hearing something about it at work. She's okay, though, right?"

I thought back to the walker I'd seen her using, then made a sound in the back of my throat. "I guess so. She's using a walker, though."

"Why do you ask?"

"Because she's my neighbor?" I offered up the obvious.

Even though that really wasn't the reason why. I was just a curious bastard that wanted to know more about the beautiful woman I'd seen.

The beautiful woman with her long, flowing auburn hair, her bright green eyes, and strong, muscular legs.

Legs that looked like they'd been in even better shape once upon a time.

She had generous breasts, a perfect figure that made my dick hard, and a 'don't get near me' vibe that I'd felt the moment her eyes landed on mine.

"Got it," he said. "I'll ask Audrey if she knows more. I think she said something about working with her, but I'm not quite sure."

Audrey was Fender's wife, and she was a nurse at the county hospital. If Winnie worked there, that meant she was a medical professional of some kind.

I knew she wasn't a PA or a doctor. Otherwise her kid wouldn't have to be stealing right now to resort to getting new headphones.

A nurse, maybe?

Whatever it was, I wasn't sure. But I damn sure was going to find out.

There was something about Winnifred "Winnie" Holyfield that was tugging at me, forcing me to play a game that I knew I didn't have a chance at winning.

But I was not one who didn't give it his all.

I was going to get down to the bottom of this. I was going to find out what put those shadows in her haunted eyes. And I was going to kick Matt's ass if he had anything to do with putting them there.

Because Winnie Holyfield had just gotten under my skin.

She'd been there since I'd seen the look in her eyes as she walked past her ex-husband at the grocery store. And she just dug herself deeper a few short minutes ago when she pleaded with her eyes for me not to push her further than she was willing to go yet.

CHAPTER 3

Coffee: the difference between saying 'fuck yeah' and 'fuck this.'
-Coffee Cup

Steel

Round two came two days later, only this time Conleigh was caught by a clerk when she'd tried to steal a pair of shoes.

Not shoes in her size, either. A pair in the size of a young boy.

My heart melted at the same time it seized.

Walking into the store, I went up to the cashier, paid for the shoes, and then grabbed the girl by the bicep.

She was skinny—too skinny—and that wasn't a good thing, either.

Once I deposited her in the seat of my cruiser, the front seat this time, I took a detour to McDonald's before heading to her house.

"What do you want?"

Conleigh's wide, fearful eyes turned to me.

"Uhhh," she hesitated. "A double cheeseburger off the dollar menu?"

My eye twitched.

"You want a drink?"

She licked her lips, and I could see that she'd love a drink.

"What kind?"

"Uhhh, a small sweet tea?"

I waited until we were next in line, then ordered five double cheeseburgers, three large fries, two large sweet teas, and a shit ton of ketchup.

I wasn't ashamed. I ate a lot of fuckin' ketchup.

Also, I didn't like tomatoes. Never had, and likely never would.

"Is…is some of that for you?"

I grinned. "Yeah."

"Good." She swallowed.

We didn't say anything more until she was handed her food about two minutes later.

"They're so fast," she whispered as her eyes lit on the bag of food.

"They're new," I explained. "With them being new, they're going to try really hard. Then, eventually, the new will wear off, and they'll slow down, start fucking up orders. Shit like that." Then I winced. "Sorry, I'm not used to a kid being around me."

She started to laugh. "If you only knew."

I wish I knew.

"Only knew what?"

"What my life is like."

She ate her hamburger, but her gaze kept drifting longingly toward the fries, and I snorted. "Eat them. I didn't buy all this for me."

She did, scarfing them down like only a teenager who had no problems with her metabolism could.

I'd be paying for this hamburger and fries later with about a mile per French fry, but it'd be worth it. There was nothing better than shitty food to make you forget what ails ya.

And it obviously did for her, too, because by the time I dropped her back at school—where she damn well should have been instead of out stealing shoes—she was in a chatty mood.

"My mother can't afford anything. Least of all a meal out or these shoes for my brother."

I didn't say anything to that. *Couldn't.* Mostly because she kept talking, not letting me get a word in edgewise.

"My mom had me when she was sixteen, and not long after that she got herself nationally certified as a paramedic. Only, with first me, and then my brother. She hasn't been able to work on an ambulance. Unfortunately, she has to work at the hospital, and they make a whole lot less money there. Then there's the fact that my ex-stepfather doesn't pay child support. Which then turns into my mom doing it all on her own...except she can't afford anything else because there's not enough money."

She swallowed. "I want to get a job, but there's nobody here that's hiring. Without a car, I can't drive to another city. I'm sorry I stole. I'm sorry. I couldn't help it, though. I can't stand to see my baby brother with those stupid old shoes. He's needed a new pair for a really long time. Months at least. I know my mother cries at night. I hear her."

I gritted my teeth.

"And the only thing that used to make her happy was running, and she can't even do that anymore with all her medical bills racking up due to her stroke."

"Conleigh?"

"Yeah?" she croaked.

"You can't skip school. Did you know that your mother could go to jail for you being truant?"

Her mouth fell open.

"I'm on lunch. I would've made it back in time to get to my next class. I'm never not in class. Even when I'm sick."

I grinned. "Good. But for future reference, should you ever think differently, the school can file that against your mother. So, be mindful of the choices you make, okay?"

She nodded.

I gestured to the shoes. "Take those with you, and if you ever need anything, there are other ways of getting it. I guarantee it. If you don't think there's any other way, call me."

"I don't have a phone…at least not one with any minutes on it."

I grinned. "I'm pretty sure you can find one that you can borrow. You call me if you need me."

I passed her one of my cards that was in the dash of my cruiser.

It read *Steel Cross, Chief of Police.*

"You're the chief of police?" she whispered, horrified.

I winked at her. "You got the top boss, honey. You should be happy."

She looked anything but happy. She now looks terrified.

"The offer stands, Conleigh. If you need me, call me. Okay?"

She swallowed, nodded, and then got out of the cruiser.

She was about to shut the door when she halted and turned, her eyes once again meeting mine.

"Thank you for the food. For the headphones. And the shoes. Cody will love you forever."

I smirked. "Tell him that I take payment in the form of colored pictures."

She smiled, then shut the door quietly before rushing into the school, the shoes clutched tightly to her chest.

I watched her go all the way in, then parked and got out.

I walked into the school, waving at the office ladies on the way to the school resource officer's office.

He looked up when I appeared in the doorway.

"Yo," he said, looking confused. "What are you doing here?"

Matt Holyfield, Conleigh's stepfather, and a man who had always gotten on my nerves.

"Matt," I said, coming inside. "We got a problem."

He listened as I spoke about the girl, Conleigh.

"So, what's the problem?" Matt asked. "If she's not doing it at school, there's not really much I can do on my end."

I narrowed my eyes.

"The problem is that I need to keep that girl in line, and I need to keep an eye on her. Her mom's going through a rough patch, and I'd rather not have her fall into the deep end with no floaties. Gave her my information if she ever needed help, but I'd like her to contact you if anything else gets out of hand."

Matt's lips twitched. But not in a smiling kind of way. In a 'you've got to be fucking joking' kind of way.

What the fuck was going on here?

"I'm here."

I pounded once on his desk with my fist, not using my voice because I knew that I was about to tell the fucker to get the fuck out.

God, I hated the guy.

"All right, my next stop is her mom's place. Wish me luck."

Matt snorted. "Good luck doing anything with that cun—ugh, woman. She's batshit crazy."

I didn't reply to that.

Winnie, at least in my dealings with her, hadn't been crazy.

She'd been conscientious, sad and over-worked.

What she had not been was crazy.

She hadn't yelled and screamed at Conleigh—and I'd been listening to them for weeks now because they liked to keep their windows open, and I did, too.

"Language, Matt," I growled. "And let me know if you hear anything more about Conleigh."

Matt gave me a lazy two finger salute, and I knew I wouldn't be hearing anything from the little shit.

Thoughts on who I could use to replace him if he wasn't doing his job, I stopped by the office on my way out and had a little chat with the principal.

He hadn't personally had any dealings with Matt, but that wasn't to say that he was doing any good, either.

I walked out of the school with a lot on my mind, and a lot of it had to do with the woman that I was going to see.

My last stop was Winnie's place, hoping that she would be home at lunchtime rather than at work.

I wasn't disappointed. She was at home.

I got out of my cruiser, walked up the same still-in-need-of-a-mow lawn, and knocked on the front door.

It took her much longer this time to answer the door.

"Ummm," she hesitated, looking like she'd just woken from a nap. "What are you doing here?"

She looked scared like I was going to tell her that she was being arrested.

I winced.

"I had another run-in with your girl today."

Her shoulders slumped.

"Really?" she whispered. "Did she...what happened?"

"What happened was that she tried to steal a pair of shoes for your son and got caught doing it by the store manager. After picking her up, I dropped her back off at school."

Her mouth fell open.

"You're joking."

I shook my head.

"Fuck," she whispered, then sighed and stepped back. "Come in."

I did, and she closed the door behind me.

Today she was using a cane.

It made me wonder if she had good days and bad days, or if maybe she was just getting better day by day.

I wanted to ask her about the spinal stroke, and whether or not she was going to recover, but I didn't want to overstep my bounds.

She turned and walked into the kitchen, her eyes glancing at the monitor on the table before she sighed and took a seat.

My eyes lit on the woman's backside, and all my breath stalled in my chest.

She was an older version of the girl. She for sure could've passed as her sister.

Hot damn, was she breathtaking.

"My ex-husband, the one I saw you in the store with a few weeks ago?"

Matt Holyfield.

"Yeah."

"He's the reason Conleigh is the way she is." She sighed. "When we split, she just changed. It's like her light went out, and another one, a darker one, turned on."

I'd seen that before. It was fairly common amongst youth.

"And what does Matt say about this?"

"Matt doesn't say anything because he doesn't talk to us anymore," she murmured. "Last week at the grocery store was the first time any of us, including the kids, have seen him in well over three months."

For some reason, an almost irrational amount of anger overcame me.

Matt wasn't my favorite officer by a long shot. In fact, it was safe to say that he was my least favorite of any of the men or women in my employ.

We weren't a huge metropolis with a bustling police department, but we had twenty-two officers, and five about to be sworn in straight out of the police academy. Out of all of them, Matt was the one guy who I had never liked.

Not everyone shared my opinion, though. He was well liked amongst the other officers, so I'd just written off my dislike for the man as being an isolated kind of thing.

Apparently, I was right for thinking the way I did.

I didn't like that Matt didn't have anything to do with his kids.

Now, I wanted to know why. I was curious by nature, and this would literally kill me if I didn't know.

Why I needed to know, I wasn't quite sure. Likely it was due to the girl's face when I'd caught her red-handed. Or, quite possibly, it was the fact that Winnifred—Winnie—had looked so heartbroken at hearing what her daughter had done.

Then again, it might very well be that I found her attractive as fuck.

No matter what the reason, I was going to find out.

Lani Lynn Vale

CHAPTER 4

Pepsi and Coke can't even be on the same menu together, and you want world peace?
-Steel to a fellow officer

Steel

"It's your girl again," the dispatcher said over my cell phone.

I cursed. "You're joking."

"Afraid not," she cooed. "But this one is for disorderly conduct. Not because she was trying to slip something into her coat."

There was that, at least.

I debated calling Winnie like she'd asked me to do but then decided against it. I'd seen her leave this morning on the way to leave myself. She'd given me a timid wave, and I'd waved back as I'd gotten in my car. Then I watched her struggle to get into her car, wondering idly if she'd thought about trading it in. I immediately dismissed that because if Conleigh was stealing shoes, then I doubted she had the ability to trade her car in on something easier to get into. Then again, if she was stubborn like me, it was likely that she wanted to struggle. She wanted to get better. One day she would get better and then she'd be able to get into her vehicle easily again.

I'd cursed as I'd watched her nearly fall. Then cursed some more when she left and I saw her wiping tears off her face.

So no, I wouldn't call her. I'd make sure that she heard afterward, but I wouldn't be bothering her at work.

Which led me to the goddamn mall. The mall where about fifty young kids were gathered in a circle looking at something in the middle of that circle. My guess was that in the middle of that circle would be Conleigh.

I parked as close as I dared, got out, and immediately locked the cruiser. I could just see one of these dumbass kids trying to steal it.

Little fuckers.

I pushed through the throng of young kids. They started to push me back out, but then saw who it was they were pushing. Then they started backing away.

"Sorry," one kid grumbled. "I didn't know it was you."

I snorted.

All the kids in this town knew me. All of them. I was a very visible member of the population. But I was also the president of the Dixie Wardens MC. Not to mention I started neighborhood watches. Did patrols and generally made my presence known by showing my face at all sporting events at the local high school.

"Yeah," I said. "How about you go home?"

The kid didn't argue. He just turned around and left.

Though, that might have to do with the fact that he was another cop's son. He knew when he could and couldn't joke around with me. This time being one of those times that he couldn't.

"Yes, sir."

Then he was gone and I was pushing back through more kids.

And there was Conleigh.

She and another girl the same age were screaming at each other.

"Your mother is a whore!" the other girl screamed.

"No," Conleigh disagreed. "She's not. My mother is not a whore and has never been a whore."

My eyelid twitched.

"She cheated on your father. Everybody knows Officer Holyfield would never leave your mother if she hadn't."

Yeah. Those kids loved "Officer Holy."

"No," Conleigh snapped. "My mother wasn't the cheater. My stepfather was. Go ask Cohen's mom."

"My boyfriend's mom didn't cheat with Officer Holy. Fuck you."

I sighed.

"Girls," I growled. "Time to break it up. It's time for you all to leave."

That last part I said loudly. Loud enough that every single one of the little shits had heard it.

They shuffled from foot to foot, unwilling to leave the juicy gossip.

"Now!"

Most of them left. But they didn't go far.

"Girls," I said. "What's going on?"

"She's spreading rumors about my mother," Conleigh snarled. "Saying she's a whore and that she deserves to be poor. She won't stop talking about her, and now everyone at school thinks I'm 'just like my mother.'"

I gritted my teeth and turned my eyes toward the other girl.

"What's your name?"

The girl didn't immediately answer. Conleigh did, though.

"Shannon Noor."

Shannon's eyes narrowed, and I saw her body tense in readiness.

"If you hit her, I will take you to jail for assault."

The girl took a hasty step back.

"Time to go home."

The girl gave Conleigh one more long glare and then swiveled around with the amount of anger that only a hormonal teenager could've pulled it off.

Conleigh glared at her back the entire way.

"Let's go."

She didn't argue, and it was only when we were in my cruiser that I saw why.

She was crying silently beside me.

I had no clue what to say.

"My son, Sean," I finally settled on. "Is getting calls from my ex. She's a whore. I know whores. Your mother is not one."

Conleigh burst out laughing in between sobs.

"Thanks for that," she said as she wiped her eyes.

"Why do you keep doing this?" I asked. "One of these days I'm not going to be on duty and you're going to get picked up by one of my cops that doesn't have a soft spot for pain in the ass girls. He's gonna take you into the station and book you. Then you're going to forever have a record. Do you know what that does to you when you try to get a job?"

She stubbornly didn't reply.

I sighed and started my cruiser, backing out of the crowd of people who were still gathered. Before I left all the way, I stopped and picked up my mic that would allow me to speak over the loudspeaker.

"In ten minutes I'm going to have a unit come over and make sure this parking lot is clear of loiterers. And, for all of you peabrains that don't know what a loiter is, that would be the ones that are still standing around in the parking lot. If you're still here, he's going to be handing out tickets. Fines for said tickets are two hundred and thirty bucks. They also can't be dropped. Think about that."

Before I'd even hung the mic up, people were dispersing.

"Are they really that much money?"

I grinned. "No. They're about seventy-five. But these kids don't know that."

Conleigh grinned at me. The grin quickly fell.

"I gotta tell you something." She licked her lips and then looked away.

"What?"

I waited and listened as I maneuvered out of the mall parking lot, making it nearly halfway to her house before she decided to speak again.

When she did, my gut twisted.

"My dad—stepdad—cheated on my mom."

I winced.

"With her best friend."

My brows rose. "You know that for sure?"

I hadn't heard a damn thing, and the station was a damn gossip mill.

She nodded, swallowing convulsively. "I heard her crying when she was packing our things when we moved out of Matt's house. That girl, Krisney, the one we rented the house from?"

I nodded.

"She was asking mom what happened. My mom thought I was at school, but I'd walked home because it was early release and she forgot. Anyway, Mom was telling Krisney that my stepfather cheated on her with her best friend. And her best friend at the time's husband was dying of cancer. Apparently, it was going on for a really, really long time."

I felt sick to my stomach.

"I was hoping if I could do something bad…bad enough that the cops came, that one of those times Matt would come."

"And what were you going to say to Matt?"

She pursed her lips, and her eyes changed. Before I could say anything on that, though, a call came in. I held up my hand when she started to reply to my question, and she clamped her mouth shut.

"All units be advised, there is a white male in a white t-shirt and baggy jeans walking down the middle of 240…he's been flashing passing motorists his privates. Ummm, he's also been pressing his genitalia against car windows that are stopped at stoplights."

I bit my lip and momentarily closed my eyes.

"Does that mean he's pressing his dick to people's windows?"

I snorted. "Yes."

"Can you go pick him up? That's like half a block from here!"

I immediately shook my head. "No. I'm not dragging you to a call like that. Someone else will pick him up."

"Please?"

I shook my head.

"All units be advised, the subject just exposed himself to a child by pressing his genitals into a cracked car window. The driver rolled his, ummm, genitalia up in the window."

Conleigh burst out laughing, her hand smacking hard against her thigh.

But she got her wish.

With me being that close to the scene, I couldn't just leave.

I parked next to the car that had the guy's dick rolled up in the window and immediately recognized the vehicle. It belonged to one of the old ladies—Truth's.

"Don't get out of this car," I ordered Conleigh. "Once another unit arrives on scene, we'll leave. Understand?"

She nodded her head and held up her pinky. "Pinky promise."

I winked at her, took her pinky with mine, and shook it lightly before letting it go. "Be good. Don't press any buttons."

Conleigh grinned. I slammed the door and went to deal with the poor schmuck who thought he could put his dick into a mama bear's window.

Shit.

Before rounding the car, I sent out a quick text to Truth.

BP (11:59 AM): I'm here. Don't freak out.

I knew that Verity, Truth's wife, had already sent a text message.

Her phone was in her hand, and her child, EJ, was in her arms.

She was glaring at the man who was busy screaming his head off about his balls hurting.

Truth (11:59 AM): I'm on my way.

I rolled my eyes.

Of course, Truth was freaking out.

I sighed and walked to Verity, who was now standing a bit away from the car due to the man's incessant crying.

"You okay?"

She nodded.

EJ leaned over, and I grinned as I took him into my arms.

"You okay, boy?"

EJ nodded his head.

He was nothing like his father. He wasn't outspoken, but he was very watchful and curious. He loved Verity so much that it hurt to watch sometimes.

Made me realize what my own son had missed growing up with a mother like her.

"Give me a hug, boyo. I have to go deal with the trash."

EJ gave me a hug, and I handed him back to Verity before giving her a wink. "Nice job. But you might want to take this a little further away. Truth is on his way."

Verity rolled her eyes, but she did as I said seeing as both of us knew what would happen when he got there.

He was going to blow the fuck up, and Truth didn't fuck around. When he blew up, he blew up big.

I sighed and turned back to the man whose dick and balls were rolled up in the car window and wondered idly whether or not I should take him out without backup present.

Deciding that that wouldn't be a good idea since I couldn't assure myself that the flasher wouldn't run, I waited until another cruiser showed up on the scene. Tough, an officer that had been with us for going on ten years now, stepped out.

He took one look at the car, saw Verity off to the side, and then burst out in guffaws.

"Shit," the big black man, one of the best officers we had in the entire state, rubbed his tears away. "I just...I just should've known it'd be one of your old ladies. You boys and your girls."

I didn't disagree. The entire club was now married. Every man in it had a great woman on the back of their bikes—except me—and all of those women were crazy. Crazy in a good way, but crazy nonetheless.

"Shut it, Tough," I muttered under my breath. "Get over here and get ready to catch him. I'm fairly sure once blood flow returns to his boys, he's going to hit his knees. But I'm not one hundred percent certain of it, so be ready if he tries to run."

Tough gave me a half-hearted salute, then went to stand behind the man.

He didn't get too close.

Then again, he didn't need to.

Tough was one fast motherfucker.

He was big, but he also had the speed of an NFL tight end. He might look slow, but goddamn would he ever surprise you.

I'd raced him one time—and one time only—and wound up eating his dust.

Dropping halfway into Verity's car, I'd just turned the ignition on and reached for the windows when two things happened.

One, Winnie stepped out of her car and started to yell at her daughter. Her daughter that was busy laughing her ass off and taking pictures of the stupid man with his dick and balls stuck in the window.

Two, Truth pulled up with the roar of screeching tires and a revving engine. He stopped his bike at the front of Verity's car, got off of it and started stalking toward the poor motherfucker who definitely chose the wrong fucking car.

I sighed and hit the button to roll the window down.

The Flasher hit his knees, but he was right back up again when he saw Truth heading for him.

It wouldn't surprise me if the Flasher knew who Truth was. Everyone did. We were members of the Dixie Wardens MC. It was hard not to know who each of us were if you lived in this town.

It's not like we weren't well known. We were. The Rejects did a lot of volunteering and held a lot of parties. We did a lot of everything, really.

And Truth was in the spotlight just as much as I was at times.

Especially after his swordsmith skills were mentioned in the fucking *NY Times* newspaper just last month.

Truth might be well known…but he honestly didn't care. Especially when, after seeing the stupid man trying to run, he went after him.

Truth caught him. Tough hadn't even bothered to go after him, knowing it wouldn't be necessary.

"Truth…"

Truth slammed his fist into the stupid man's face, dropped him like a sack of flour, and then turned on his heel to go to his wife.

His son threw himself into his arms the moment he got within reach, and Verity wrapped herself around him.

And my heart started to ache.

"Why are you here, Conleigh Annaliese?"

I pinched the bridge of my nose and waved my hand. "Picked her up."

Winnie's eyes never strayed off her daughter. "And what happened this time?"

I felt someone come up beside me. Tough.

He watched the mother and daughter square off toward each other just as I was doing.

"This is Matt Holyfield's ex-wife," Tough whispered. "Holy shit. Why do you have his kid in your cruiser?"

I grimaced. "Long story."

"Long story that I want to hear over a beer tonight," he ordered.

And it *was* an order. He wouldn't rest until he knew the full story, and I knew it.

"Fine. The usual spot?"

He nodded. "I'm gonna take that poor guy to the clink. I'll see you around eight when our shift ends."

And then Tough left, leaving me with two very pissed off girls in the middle of the road, staring at each other. Neither one of them willing to back down.

A car horn honked, reminding me that we were, indeed, in the middle of a freakin' street blocking three of the five lanes of traffic.

"Ladies," I said, voice tired. "Take it to the shoulder. Truth! Come move this car and your bike!"

"Get in the car," Winnie growled.

And then I saw her limping to her car, sans cane or walker.

It made me smile.

"All my stuff is in Steel's cruiser."

Winnie growled. "Get your stuff, then meet me in that parking lot. I'll pick you up there."

Then Winnie was in her car, her eyes angry, as she moved out of the road.

She'd just pulled into the closest parking lot and parked when another cruiser arrived on scene.

This one was not welcome.

Matt poked his head out and then offered me a mocking grin.

"Darn, I'm sorry I didn't get here sooner," he lied.

I knew he was lying, too. *Fucker.*

Conleigh rounded my car then and walked up to where I was just making my way to the shoulder.

"Conleigh, what are you doing here?"

Conleigh ignored Matt, turning her eyes completely to me.

"Conleigh."

"Thank you for the ride," she said, her eyes sliding away from me momentarily to Matt who'd said her name once again. "I appreciate your words of wisdom and your understanding."

I touched the tip of her nose. "Go before your mother freaks out."

Conleigh grinned, then purposefully walked behind my cruiser to avoid getting any closer to Matt, who was staring at her, watching her go.

I drew Matt's attention when I said, "What are you doing here?"

"I just came off lunch," he murmured. "Wanted to make sure you had it all in hand."

Sure, he did.

It wasn't a coincidence, and it didn't escape my attention, that he always showed up to a scene *after* everything was all said and done.

He'd been doing that for about six months now, and it was starting to get on my goddamn nerves.

I assigned him to the school as the resource officer as a last resort. He picked up very little overtime and still managed to swap quite a few shifts with other officers. Meaning that half the time he wasn't at the school dealing with the students, building relationships with them and performing his duties as the resource officer like he was supposed to be doing.

But since I allowed the officers under my command to do that at will, as long as the required number of officers were on shift, and not a lot of overtime was being had, I couldn't exactly argue that he did it. Mostly because then it would be known amongst everyone that I didn't care for the fucker.

"It's all in hand," I said as Truth backed his bike off the street.

Once it was safely ensconced behind my cruiser, he went to move Verity's car, but not before sneering slightly at Matt.

Good to know it isn't just me.

"Who did you swap with for today?" I questioned.

It may sound like curiosity, but I truly needed to know who was switching with whom. Normally I got at least a text message saying who was taking whose shift. It hadn't happened with Matt, though.

Then again, I hadn't made it mandatory, and since Matt didn't do anything he didn't have to do, it shouldn't surprise me.

"Harrison," Matt answered instantly.

I rolled my eyes skyward. "For which shift next week?"

"Monday and Tuesday."

I growled under my breath.

"I know that I've told you before that you need to be a little more consistent than you're being. Those kids up there need a resource officer that they can turn to when they need one. You, of all people, should know that they need consistency," I said in a very even tone.

Matt's eye twitched. "Is that why my daughter is here?" he asked, sounding a little put out. "Her mom wouldn't like to know that you brought her daughter to a scene like that. She's protective."

What mother wouldn't be?

And I hardly had a choice where I brought her when a call like that came in.

Before I could tell him that Winnie was already well aware of the situation, another call came in. This one being a minor wreck two blocks over. "How about you go get that one…since you're so close."

And, since he couldn't very well argue with the chief of police and keep his job, Matt nodded once stiffly and started down the road.

"You really are pissing that one off," Tough said thoughtfully from behind me.

I'd known he was there, but since he was busy writing up a report, I hadn't thought much about him overhearing what I had to say.

Anything I said to Matt were things I'd say in public or in private. Just like I'd do with all of my officers if the situation warranted it.

"That one gets on my nerves," I felt comfortable enough to say.

Tough was the captain of our band of misfits at the police station. He knew all that went on just as well as I did.

"That one gets on everybody's nerves but Harrison's," Tough countered.

"Good to know it's not just me," I muttered, then glanced into Tough's car. "Is he asleep?"

Tough grunted. "Sure the fuck is. He got in there and laid down like it was his own personal car. So, I figured I'd stay and listen to what was going on with that douche canoe instead of writing this report at the station."

I snorted. "You never miss the chance to catch the gossip, Tough."

Tough burst out laughing. "I gotta tell the wife something when I get home. And, I got something juicy today. Don't think I didn't miss those heated stares between you and Douche Canoe's ex-wife."

"She was just mad," I countered.

"Mad and horny. For you."

I didn't have anything to say to that.

"She's not in the place right now to handle what I got on my plate," I muttered. "Take care. I gotta go to the girl's house and have a talk with that same mother. I have to explain why she was here with me."

Tough found that hilarious. "You ever thought of calling?"

My eye twitched. "Yeah, but why bother when I gotta go home anyway, and she lives across the street? Seems counterproductive when I could just run over there real quick."

"She's your neighbor?" Tough's smile widened. "Oh, my Leilan is going to love this!"

Ignoring him, I walked to my cruiser and drove away without deigning to reply to his comment.

Tough was worse than a high school girl.

Seriously, I think he could drama Conleigh under the table.

Arriving at my house minutes later, I pulled into my driveway and went straight to Winnie's house instead of my own.

The screams coming from inside were loud enough to permeate through the closed door.

I knocked, wondering if anyone would even hear.

Conleigh answered a few moments later, looking like she was about ten seconds away from pulling her hair out.

"She went to the store," Conleigh murmured. "But she'll be right back. We only needed milk. As long as you don't mind listening to my brother screech at the top of his lungs…"

"What's wrong with your brother?"

"My brother's pissed off at the world today and letting everybody know it."

I walked into a warzone.

CHAPTER 5

*Do you ever wake up and think you're not really in the mood for
human interaction that day, or is it just me?*
-Text from Winnie to Steel

Winnie

5 hours earlier

"Have fun at the mall, baby," I said to Conleigh as I dropped her
off in the front of Sears.

Conleigh grunted. "I'm going to look for a job while I'm here."

I didn't argue with that.

She could look all she wanted, but she needed a place she could
work that she could get to without a car, and the mall wasn't one of
those places.

"I'll see you at four, correct?"

She and a couple of friends were watching a movie, having some
lunch, and then going to hang until I could make my way back
around to them.

I had a million and one things to do today, and all of those things
were on opposite sides of the freakin' city.

"Yeah, Mom."

Then Conleigh was gone, and I was left with a clearly excited Cody.

Cody, my five-year-old baby boy, was so excited to see his father that I could hardly get him to quiet down.

And I was a nervous wreck.

Cody hadn't been away from me, except for the odd half a day with Matt's parents, since he'd been born. Sure, he went to daycare, but daycare always meant that he spent every single night at home with me in his house.

Now, he was staying in his old room at his father's place, and I was worried that he'd like it better there than with me.

I pulled up into our designated meeting spot and clenched my teeth when I saw Angelina's car instead of Matt's Ford.

Angelina got out and started to walk over to me, leaving her own kids in her car, screaming.

Her eldest sat there, too, staring at his mother's back as she came my way.

Angelina's eldest was her first child with a different man. He'd been the reason that Angelina and I had first become friends.

Our children were the same age. Her eldest, right along with her youngest.

When I'd moved here, she'd immediately taken me under her wing. She and her husband had made me feel so welcome, that I had no choice but to love her.

She'd introduced me to Matt, her husband's best friend, and the rest had been history.

We'd always been a team.

And now we weren't.

She'd stolen something from me that was unforgivable.

I rolled down my window.

"What are you doing here?" I asked.

"Matt can't make it. He has to work today."

My eyelid twitched. "Then why didn't he call and say that?"

Angelina crossed her arms over her chest and stared back at me. "Because he still wants him to come over. He'll be home around eleven. They'll have all morning together before we have to bring him back."

Not likely. Cody slept until ten o'clock most days if he was allowed to. I highly doubted that Matt would wake Cody up. He never had before when he'd been living with us. He'd much rather go work out and do his own thing than have his son tagging along.

Which led me to my next decision.

"We'll try next weekend."

Then I rolled up my window.

Angelina looked pissed, but I ignored her.

I was not, under any circumstances, giving that woman my kid.

First of all, she didn't take care of my children well, and never had.

She was a very lax parent and didn't care what her kids did— whether that was allowing them to ride in a booster seat when they clearly should be in a car seat or stay up until three a.m. eating junk food instead of going to bed at a decent hour.

So, no, I sure as hell wasn't leaving my kid with her when I hadn't trusted her *before* she'd screwed me over.

Now that she had ruined my life, there was no way I was trusting her with what was left of it.

Conleigh and Cody were the only two things holding me together anymore, and lately, Conleigh was challenging that.

I ignored the woman who was now on her phone, probably calling her new husband, and instead drove away and headed for the grocery store.

Cody, not realizing that he wasn't going to get to see his father yet, seemed happy and content in the back seat.

"Just wasted an hour of my life I'll never get back," I grumbled to nobody in particular.

After making a grocery run, with a still happy and behaving well Cody, I headed back to the main part of the town, only to see my freakin' daughter in the middle of the road.

Staring at a man who was standing up against a car.

From this angle, I couldn't see much besides my daughter's laughing face.

Sudden and irrational anger hit me, and I pulled the car over to the side of the road and yelled at her.

"Why are you here, Conleigh Annaliese?"

Steel turned at hearing me and winced. "Picked her up."

"And what did she do this time?"

The next fifteen minutes went about as expected.

Steel explained why he'd had to intervene when it came to my child, and I had to hold my tongue while he did. Luckily, after explaining why he had Conleigh, he'd been called over due to an altercation with the naked man and an irate man who wasn't very happy at having that naked man press his genitals to his wife's window.

Using the chance to escape while I could, I gave Conleigh one single quelling stare, and she started marching toward my car.

After making sure she was settled, I ripped her a new one.

"Tell me why you were there," I demanded.

"I went to the mall."

"Yeah," I agreed. I knew that part.

"And Cohen was there with his girlfriend."

I hadn't seen the girlfriend in the car with Angelina when I'd gone to drop Cody off with Matt, but it didn't surprise me that she was in there. Angelina took the kids anywhere they wanted to go, and always had.

They must've gone straight there after I'd left.

"And…"

"And Cohen's girlfriend called you a whore, and I took offense to it."

I closed my eyes.

"Conleigh," I breathed. "With Matt being a cop, everyone knows him in the city. Since they don't want to think that a cop is one of the bad guys, they're going to find it easier to blame the other person, and that's me, unfortunately."

Conleigh didn't say anything.

"I don't want you to do anything stupid because of something they call me. I'm an adult, I can handle it…and so can you," I said softly.

Conleigh's jaw tightened and she looked away to study the very uninteresting landscape as we made our way home.

"Why do you have Cody?"

I rolled my eyes.

"Seems that Matt was working today and that Angelina was picking him up. I refused to give him to her."

"Is that legal?"

I shrugged. "We don't have any sort of formal visitation agreement. Hell, we don't even have anything registered with the court, yet. He could take me to court for custody, but I don't think he will. He's just not interested enough."

"I saw him out with his new family yesterday."

I sighed.

"Yeah, I saw them come into the hospital yesterday, too," I admitted. "He came in with the youngest because she fell off the bunk beds. Held her like he used to hold Cody. He never once asked how Cody was. Didn't even seem to care, even when I was the tech that helped clean her up. Pissed me the hell off."

"I thought you weren't supposed to talk about seeing patients."

I snorted. Conleigh lecturing me on what was right and wrong was quite comical.

"I'm not," I admitted.

"Well, it'll be our secret then."

Rolling my eyes, I drove my little family home, refusing to let my mind wander to the sexy older officer at the scene who was starting to take over my daily thoughts lately.

***

I had groceries in one hand—more than I'd intended on getting—and my purse in the other when my phone started to ring.

I grimaced when I saw who was calling.

If there was one person on this planet who I never wanted to talk to, it would be Matt.

Fucking jerk.

"Hello?" I answered as calmly as I could manage.

"Did you know that the chief of police took Conleigh to a scene today that was volatile?"

Volatile?

I would hardly call some man's dick being rolled up in a car window volatile.

"I was there, yes," I answered breathlessly. "He didn't take her to a scene on purpose. He was bringing her home from the mall."

At least, that was what Conleigh had told me on the way home.

I hadn't gotten much info on it before Cody had started throwing the world's worst temper tantrum.

He wanted his daddy.

The daddy who'd neglected to pick him up today like he'd said he would.

"Well, she saw some guy's dick and balls," Matt fumed.

Fumed.

What. The. Fuck?

"Matt, did you forget that you were picking Cody up today?"

"I sent Angelina."

I knew that.

"Yes, but if you're not going to pick him up, which is something we've discussed before, then I'm not giving him to Angelina. She doesn't watch the kids well enough for me to allow her to have my child," I said carefully, trying not to let Winnie the Shrew out to play.

"Angelina watches her kids," he contradicted me.

"Then why did you have a child fall off the bunk beds, and your new wife say that she hadn't been watching them?" I countered. "Which was just a few days ago."

Matt grunted. "I was calling to talk to you about the Chief taking our girl to that scene today."

Our girl.

Now *that* made me mad.

He'd never called Conleigh his. Had never even offered to adopt her or give her his name. All of which I was grateful for now, but still.

"Conleigh is sixteen, Matt. She has a good head on her shoulders, and Steel is very nice. He wouldn't have taken her to a scene if he thought she could be hurt. Trust me."

"I've heard that she's been bad lately. In fact, Steel," he sounded like he sneered. "Came in to tell me that I needed to keep a better eye on her because she was acting strangely."

I was sure there was more to it than that, but I wasn't going to get that information out of Matt.

Nor did I particularly want to talk to him.

"Well, thanks," I said breezily. "I have to go, though."

Matt started to say something more, but I was having none of it and hung up.

Fucker.

I picked up the groceries, held my purse in my hand and shoved my phone in my bra, then started up the steps of the house.

I used the railing as I went since I'd left the cane back in my car and breathed a sigh of relief when I made it.

However, when it came to a door, I knew it was a lost cause. There was no way that I could maneuver into that opening without holding on to the threshold.

Placing the groceries down on the stoop, I pushed open the door until I could fit through.

The first thing I noticed as I entered was the lack of yelling from Cody versus when I left.

Which made me smile.

Cody loved Conleigh.

And then I heard the low murmur of voices.

Frowning, I peeked around the corner of the entryway.

The last thing I expected when I got home was to find the sexy officer in my kitchen. Though, I guess it shouldn't have surprised me. Not with Conleigh's grabby hands lately.

God, the sexiest man alive was sitting at my kitchen table, and that was only because my daughter was becoming a thief!

Holy shit!

I watched as the officer's fingers flew over the keyboard of the phone. For a sexy older man with large hands, he was surprisingly adept at texting.

I shuffled carefully, feeling good today after the latest twelve-hour shift, and came to a stop right outside the kitchen as I leaned against the door and carefully toed off my shoes.

As I did, I listened to what was going on in my kitchen.

"What are you doing?"

"Checking up on Matt." The police chief, Steel, grinned. "I sent a text message to my son, then to Fender, to find out what they knew about Matt."

Conleigh's frown furrowed even deeper.

"But what are you going to do?"

"I'm going to check into him," he repeated, not really giving her much information.

Which also meant not giving *ME* any more information.

"What the hell?" I murmured.

Why were they looking up Matt?

Then Conleigh started to talk again.

"I can tell you everything you want to know about the lying bi— woman."

Steel's lips twitched. "I'm not sure I should be having this conversation with you."

I wasn't either.

Then again, it wasn't her story to tell. It was mine.

I stepped into the room and made myself known to the room's two awake occupants. The one sleeping occupant was Cody, who was asleep in Steel's arms—causing my heart to melt.

"Why are you looking into my ex-husband?"

Steel looked up, spotting me in the doorway, and stood.

"Mrs. Holyfield…"

I held up my hand. "You need to stop."

Steel's eyes narrowed.

"I didn't mean to step on any toes…"

"Mom…"

"I have to get Cody started on his bath," I murmured.

Conleigh beat me to it.

She walked up to Steel, taking Cody's limp body in her arms, and then rushed out of the room before I could tell her I'd do it.

I sighed and turned back to Steel, my ex's boss.

Some people called him Big Papa, but I wasn't sure I could ever call him that.

It was awkward. Especially when he kept bringing my delinquent daughter back to me.

"Ma'am…" He hesitated, starting toward me.

I held up a hand.

"He cheated on me."

He paused in the middle of my kitchen floor.

"He what?"

I nodded. "He cheated on me."

It was obvious that he wasn't going to back down. For some reason, this man really wanted to know why Conleigh was having trouble. And for some reason, I felt like telling him.

I didn't have anybody to talk to anymore. I'd not only lost my husband when he'd cheated on me, but I'd lost my best friend as well. My best friend who'd cheated on her husband—her dying husband—with my husband.

"I'm sorry."

I shrugged.

"Is it because of your legs?"

I looked down at my feet, as I eased on my fluffy blue pair of slippers which had been lying in the hallway.

"No." I paused. "It gets worse, though."

"I don't see how." He admitted as he took a seat, leaning back in his chair and crossing his arms over his chest.

I laughed humorlessly.

"I found out that my husband was cheating on me when my child told me."

"What?"

I nodded. "My youngest."

His confusion was obvious, and I smiled, but it didn't meet my eyes.

"He kept saying 'Daddy likes her kisses' to my best friend, Angelina. He'd pull her hand and pull her over to my ex-husband." I cleared my throat. "They laughed it off like it wasn't happening, but I got curious one day when I walked over to their house and found nobody home."

"Okay…"

I waved my hand in the air.

"My best friend and her husband, Mark, lived across the street from us. They bought their house about a year after we'd bought ours. It was the perfect set-up…until Mark was diagnosed with testicular cancer." She scratched her head. "It had been caught too late, and it had already spread to his lymph nodes. By the time they realized there was something wrong, it was in his chest and blood."

I swallowed through a suddenly dry throat.

"Since Mark and my ex were best friends, he was over there helping a lot. He did everything he could to help make Angelina and Mark's last days together not such a hardship."

"But…"

"But, while Mark lay in his bed dying, Angelina and Matt used the guest bedroom to fuck. One day, Matt was watching our kids, and he took them over there with him. Only, he didn't secure the door well enough, because her kids and Cody saw what happened in there. Meaning my son's 'Daddy likes her kisses' comment was said in more of a 'since I've seen you do it before' way and not in a 'do it for my entertainment' kind of way.

"The day I found out was also the day that I had a spinal stroke." I looked away. "I was in the hospital when Matt served me with divorce papers. He also went ahead and said I could keep the kid while I was at it. Something about wanting to have a family of his own with Angelina."

I could tell he didn't know what to say.

Literally, he had nothin'.

"He changed his mind on Cody later, though, when Angelina said that it wasn't nice. So now he's attempting to see Cody. Conleigh, on the other hand, is banned from her house because she thinks my daughter will be a bad influence on her son."

Steel blinked, his long eyelashes laying lightly against his upper cheek for a long moment before they opened again.

Why in the hell did men, who didn't give one damn about eyelashes, always have better ones than women?

"So he's done nothing with Conleigh since y'all have split?"

I nodded. "Right."

"No wonder she's acting out," he mused. "How long were y'all together?"

"Conleigh was eight when we met. Almost ten when we married. So, seven years altogether, six of those married," I answered, feeling a twinge deep inside my chest.

But not for my loss, for Conleigh's.

Conleigh had been Matt's little shadow since we'd met and then got married. Then, all of a sudden once I found out about Matt and Angelina's betrayal, they not only dropped me but my girl as well.

I hurt for her.

"I think he's seen her twice," I continued. "Cody, probably about twice that. That's actually one of the things I was supposed to do today with him. I was at the mall at our scheduled time to meet, Cody knew he was going to his dad's…then Angelina showed up and told me that Matt was working and that she was there in his stead."

I laughed humorlessly.

"I can see why you wouldn't want her anywhere near your kid," he mused.

He smoothed his hand down a wet spot on his shirt and smiled.

"Drool. He's been doing that for a while. I'm afraid he takes after me like that." I giggled, then sobered. "Angelina, though, isn't the most attentive of parents. She never has been. When her husband got sick, those kids went wild because nobody was containing them any longer. At least before, when her husband wasn't sick, he'd keep them semi under control. But then once he was not there as a stable force in their daily lives, all they had left was Angelina, and she just didn't care enough. I think every single one of her kids has had at least three broken bones."

His eyes widened.

"You think she's abusive?"

I shook my head. "No. Not abusive. Inattentive—she just doesn't watch them. She'll leave them alone to do what they will. She's there in body, just not in spirit, you know?"

He nodded.

"I'll keep an eye out."

"Matt's there now," I said, wincing. "At least he'll help keep them in line. That was something good that came out of it I guess."

He grunted, not agreeing with me.

I sighed and stood up. "We had it rough...*have* it a little rough...but I'm getting back on my feet. All the medical bills I accrued were paid for when Matt and I finalized the divorce. Now I'm just trying to recoup my half of the credit card bills. I'm hoping as time progresses that I can afford more things, and hopefully take a little bit of the strain off of Conleigh. Maybe if I can give her a few pretty things, she'll be able to function better at school. I'm never going to bring her stepfather back...but I can make it easier on her that way."

He didn't say anything to that, either.

So I got up and headed to the kitchen, realizing that somewhere in that discussion Conleigh had slipped in with my groceries and left again.

A sudden idea occurred to me, and I turned to find Steel studying me from behind. "You want to stay for dinner?"

I licked my lips suddenly, surprised that I'd asked him that.

It had been months since Matt and I had split and about eight weeks since our divorce was finalized. A long time since I'd had anyone else to feed besides me and my two kids.

The prospect of him staying for dinner and enjoying my cooking really appealed to me in an instinctive sort of way.

I loved taking care of people. I loved when people enjoyed my food, and honestly, I never got that from my kids.

"Sure."

I was utterly surprised to hear him say yes.

"Really?"

He nodded, then frowned. "As long as you're not planning on making anything weird."

I started to laugh. "Spaghetti isn't really weird, is it?"

He shook his head. "No."

"Good," I said as I went to the sink and washed my hands. "I just have to make the pasta."

"Make the pasta?"

I nodded and turned my body slightly so that I could see him. "I make my own pasta. It's cheaper in the long run if I make it in bulk. It'll take me about an hour…that's okay, right?"

He stood up and walked to the counter to lean his hips against it and cross his legs. "Now you have me curious. I've never had homemade pasta before."

So, I spent the next hour showing him how it was done, and then another hour making the meatballs and sauce.

"This is the best spaghetti I've ever had in my life," he informed me. "And I've eaten at Olive Garden."

I burst out laughing.

He watched me laugh, an odd look on his face.

I smiled as I calmed down. "What?"

He shook his head. "Just haven't seen you smile before. I like it."

Pleasure washed over me, but before I could reply to his words, his phone rang.

He pulled it out of his pocket and cursed, ignoring the call.

Thirty seconds later, it rang again, this time he answered it.

"Yeah, son?" He paused, eyes narrowing. "I'll call her. I told you to block her number." He brought his hand up to his face, and I stood to clear the table.

"Conleigh?" I said. "Do you think you can put the food away while I get your brother cleaned up and in bed?"

Conleigh nodded and stood, her half-empty plate in her hands. "Save yours, too. I'll take it to work tomorrow for lunch."

Conleigh looked at her plate, clearly skeptical, but nodded anyway. "Okay."

Then I went about getting Cody ready for bed and tucked in tight.

My left leg was a little weak as I made my way down the hall toward where I could hear Steel and Conleigh speaking in low tones.

"Your son is how old?"

"Thirty-four."

My brows rose.

Steel must've been young like I was when he first had his son.

"How old were you when you had him?" Conleigh asked the same question that I was thinking.

"Nineteen, almost twenty," he answered. "Still in college."

"At least you weren't sixteen like my mom."

My heart hurt.

That was true.

I also agreed with her.

Sixteen had been ridiculous. I'd gotten pregnant, and my life had completely changed. My family had disowned me, and my mother and father kicked me out the moment they found out.

I moved in with my grandparents, finished out my school year, and raised a newborn all at the same time. When I was eighteen, I moved away and never looked back.

Not that I didn't love my grandparents, but I knew just as well as they did that they didn't really want me there.

They'd felt sorry for me and took me in because they felt obligated to.

Once I was no longer in high school, I found a job, got help from the government in the form of food stamps, housing aid and help paying for my education in the form of Pell grants.

Once I graduated, I found a full-time job, got off of food stamps and into my own place, and kept on kicking ass.

Then I met Matt, and I got complacent.

"I actually got a girl pregnant when I was sixteen," he said. "She was fifteen. Lost the kid."

My brows went up at that.

"What?"

Steel started to laugh at Conleigh's surprised exclamation.

"Yep," he confirmed. "Scared me straight…at least for two more years."

I found myself smiling as I made my way into the kitchen where both of them were standing side-by-side at the sink. Steel had his hands wrist deep in the left half of the sink, washing the dishes, while Conleigh was on the right side, rinsing and drying them.

I felt my heart stutter in my chest at the sight.

I couldn't remember the last time Conleigh willingly did the dishes without me nearly crying to get her to do so.

Now she was laughing with the man I was finding it harder and harder not to think about, and I was loving every second of it.

I'm so screwed.

Lani Lynn Vale

CHAPTER 6

You want to know how lesbian sex works? Well, for starters, both
people orgasm.
-True Fact

Winnie

I rubbed my forehead in concern.

"Mom," Conleigh breathed. "I don't understand."

I didn't either.

That was the problem.

I passed algebra, calculus, physics, and, hell, even calculus two, with flying colors. Yet, I couldn't figure out what the hell to do with my daughter's tenth-grade pre-cal math homework.

I was such a loser.

"Con," I said softly. "I just don't understand. I'd have to reteach myself. Which I'm more than willing to do. However, it's going to take me more than the twenty minutes that I have before I have to leave for work."

Conleigh looked away.

"Are you sure that taking a night shift is a good idea?"

No.

Yet, I needed money. I needed to put food on my children's plates.

I needed…help.

Help that I wasn't going to find anywhere.

I'd contacted the attorney general's office yesterday about back child support for Cody.

It was a gamble.

By doing so, I was admitting that I needed help. I was also letting him know that he still had his rights as a parent, and alerting him to the fact that he could potentially take me to court to lower the child support settlement we reached in an out-of-court agreement two months ago. Child support he'd promised to deliver—the whole two months' worth—but never had.

Until that came through, I couldn't afford to not take extra shifts. Not with Christmas coming up, anyway.

I sighed inwardly at everything that I needed to do.

With her struggling with her own homework, there was no way I was going to be able to help Cody with his sight words.

"Mom!"

I looked over to see Cody standing there looking at me.

"Yeah?"

"I got papers!"

I *hated* papers.

Seriously, if I never saw another shittily—*is that even a word?* — colored fucking *paper* it'd be too soon.

"Oh, yay!" I cheered falsely. "Whatcha got?"

He gave me the papers that were haphazardly stuffed into his folder, and I winced.

He had a stack full of them.

Shit.

I dreaded the day when all my son's graded papers came home.

He was a smart cookie…except when he'd put his stubborn foot down, then all bets were off.

He was like me in that way.

Unfortunately, things didn't come easily for either of my two children.

Conleigh had been struggling since she moved to her new school district in the second grade. Cody was struggling to say the freakin' alphabet correctly every single time.

If he couldn't do the alphabet, how the hell was he supposed to grasp the concept of an actual word?

Then I saw the official-looking letter that was tucked in his folder amid all the graded papers that had been hastily shoved in there and winced.

I pulled it out and read the sticky note on top as I felt a lump form in my throat.

Winnie,

I know that we discussed this as a possibility at report card time, but I now believe he needs it for certain. Please take the time to fill out the paperwork and send it back. This is not the end of the world, I promise!

—Mrs. T.

I crumpled up the sticky note in my hand and looked at the envelope with dread.

Then I forced myself to grow a pair and opened the envelope as that lump forming in my throat grew larger.

I suspect that your son may have some developmental delays. Please don't be alarmed—it might simply be due to the fact that he did not attend pre-K. But he is lagging behind his classmates in several areas, and it would be best to address these issues now, rather than later.

I felt like throwing up.

I looked over at my son, who was now happily playing next to his toy trucks, and felt a single tear slip from my eye.

Then I sucked it up, pulled on my big girl panties, and walked to him. "Let's go over these sight words one more time."

I stopped next to Conleigh, dropped a kiss on her head and went to the chalkboard that I'd installed just for this instance.

Then, I made myself late, just so I could help my son with his sight words.

Conleigh was on her own, though.

I left my house twenty minutes later after instructing Conleigh to lock the doors and set the alarm. I headed to work with my mind all over the place.

One thing was for sure…I needed help, and I would take whatever I could get.

Little did I know that my prayers would be answered by my hot cop neighbor. And I would like it.

***

Twelve hours later

The first thing I saw when I arrived home after my night shift was my neighbor.

My thighs clenched, and I growled under my breath.

But, he wasn't where I expected him to be...like at his house, for example.

No, he was in *my* house.

Again.

It was as if he was living there.

What the hell?

I walked in with the box of donuts to find both of my kids dressed, fed and at the table.

Cody even had boots on, which was a fucking win. Normally I had to force him to put any sort of shoe on. Socks were a bonus most days.

"Uhhh," I said as I came in. "What's going on? Did something happen?"

Conleigh looked up from where she was sitting next to Steel, who was holding Cody on his lap.

Steel was fully decked out in his own uniform, my guess either coming home from work or about to go to work.

He looked a little disheveled, his hair askew a little more than his usual messy, and he had dark circles under his eyes.

"I was taking the trash out and saw Steel." Conleigh grinned. "I asked him if he happened to know how to solve quadratic equations, and he said he did. Now, here we are. I almost have my homework done."

I grinned, unable to help myself. "That's great news!"

And it was. I was happy that she was able to get her homework done. I'd spent half my night of free time trying to reteach myself how to do some of the shit that used to come so easy to me just a few short years ago.

Conleigh shot me an excited look, then looked at the clock. "I have ten minutes until the bus comes, too!"

I started to laugh.

It was fifty-fifty if we made the bus or not. Today, hopefully, they'd make it.

"Donut?"

Conleigh snickered.

"What?"

She looked at Steel, who was eyeing the room around him with laughter.

"You just offered a cop a donut," she answered.

My lips twitched. "Uhhh…I've got nothin' to say to that."

Steel stood up, setting Cody lightly on his feet.

"I'll take one of those, but I have to go. I had a call come in about five minutes ago about a cop having to go home sick. I'm gonna cover the school zone for the next hour until it ends." He looked at the kids. "I don't mind giving them a ride."

Cody whooped. "Yes!"

I rolled my eyes. "You don't have a booster seat for him."

Steel stroked his beard, bringing my attention not only to it but also to his lips.

Then he leaned forward and grabbed the box of donuts from my hands, snatching himself a chocolate one before handing the box over to Conleigh. Once Conleigh chose what she wanted, Cody pulled out the blueberry cake one, took one bite, and then put it back.

"Heard those things are easy to move around…" Steel said pointedly.

I tightened my lips together, and then nodded. "They are that."

"Then it's settled."

And then they were all loading up minutes later, but I stopped Steel before he could follow them out.

"You have crumbs," I murmured, wiping my hand down his chest.

He wasn't wearing a bullet proof vest, but his chest was hard still.

"You're not wearing a vest," I pointed out.

He winked. "I don't normally do as much running around as the rest of my officers. We purchased everyone else a ballistic vest. Mine'll be next."

And then he was walking away, but I was left reeling.

He'd made sure his entire department was outfitted with a vest before he was.

Holy shit.

That was so sweet of him, yet completely and utterly stupid.

"You're a liar from hell," I muttered to him. "How the hell are you going to tell me that you don't patrol or do anything as much as your other officers when you damn well know you've been working every single day this week."

He shrugged. "I'm older and lived a longer life. How's that?"

Terrible.

The thought of Steel dying was suddenly very unbearable for me.

"How much do these vests cost?"

I had like three hundred dollars in savings…

"Seven hundred," he answered as he took a bite of his donut. "But there are still three others I want to outfit before me, so mine'll be a while."

"You can't buy your own?" Conleigh asked.

He shrugged. "We could, but I have a mortgage payment to make, a truck payment. A grandkid, and other things I need to buy. Seven hundred dollars is better spent elsewhere."

I didn't have anything to say to that.

I didn't agree.

His grandkid could go without a toy for a couple of months…hell, so could *my* kids.

He'd used his own money on my kids, too.

Now I felt utterly like shit.

He was using his own personal money on my family, and he could be spending it on himself. Buying himself a vest that could protect his life.

I felt bile make its way up my throat.

CHAPTER 7

It's beginning to look a lot like fuck this.
-Coffee Cup

Winnie

I was walking, still without my cane, to my car where I was going to retrieve Cody's spare booster from my trunk.

We were about halfway to the driveway when Steel's words left his lips, nearly causing me to laugh.

"Why do you have a Hellcat?"

I looked at my car. My little act of rebellion. My Dodge Hellcat that Matt told me I didn't need.

"I got it because I was pissed off," I muttered, my eyes taking in the gleaming red paint, and the black racing stripe that ran down the length of it. "Two years ago, when they first came out, I told Matt how much I wanted one. He took one look at me, laughed, and then told me I couldn't handle a car like this."

I looked back over at Steel to find him grinning.

"So you got one when you broke up?"

I shook my head. "No. I got one the next week, thinking I'd show Matt. I did. He got really, *really* pissed. Then he tried to take it back. Since my name was the only one on the note, they wouldn't do anything without my say so. Pissed him off greatly, and I think ultimately that was the first fork in the road that led him to start cheating on me."

I was also upside-down on the note, and probably would be for the foreseeable future.

Steel had nothing to say to that, so I chose to continue.

"It came with two keys. A black key, and a red key," I told him.

I knew he'd ask. It never took them long.

"And what's the difference?"

"The difference is that the black key is just the normal key. With it, it drives like the next step down model would. But the red key is the—well—*key*." I grinned.

"And what does the red key do?" He came to a stop beside my car and touched the Hellcat symbol on the driver's side door, dropping down onto his haunches to do it.

"The red key is what turns the supercharger on," I explained. "And I haven't ever ridden with it before. I'm literally nervous that if I get the red key out, I'll get a ticket for going a hundred and fifty on the highway."

Steel burst out laughing. "Oh, darlin'."

I grinned and popped the trunk, gesturing for Steel to take the booster seat.

Once he had it, he walked with it to his cruiser and opened the back door.

I grinned as I saw him strap it onto the seat with the tethers.

"You do that often?" I questioned.

"Every fucking Tuesday," he answered. "I'm the car seat expert at the precinct. Since I'm certified and the other guys aren't, I'm usually the one that runs out there to check it if I'm there. There are a few others that are certified throughout the PD, but most of the time they just tell whomever it is to come back when I'm there."

I smiled. "That's actually kind of cute."

He shot me a look that clearly said what he thought of me saying he was 'cute.'

But he was. In his uniform, even it being slightly wrinkled from his day (or night, technically, depending on which way you looked at it) he was very cute.

Sexy.

Very sexy.

So sexy that sometimes I thought about him when I got my shower.

Yeah…I couldn't wait for the kids to go to school.

"Thank you again for taking them," I said just as the front door burst open, the door handle hitting the wall with Cody's exuberance to ride in a 'real life police car.'

Steel's eyes crinkled at the edges when he smiled. "Not a problem, since I'm already going over there anyway."

And then he had my kids packed in his cruiser, and moments later I had the house to myself.

I walked back inside and got a couple hours of sleep, but not before I took my shower.

Where my magical shower head was.

My magical shower head that I was now calling Steel.

Temporarily.

For now.

Not.

I was such a fucking liar.

***

It was a nearly six hours later in town that I saw Sean, Steel's son.

I'd just picked Conleigh and Cody up early from school to get their flu shots, and I was standing in the middle of the doctor's office parking lot.

"Conleigh, take Cody inside and get yourselves signed in," I ordered.

Conleigh did as she was instructed, taking Cody by the hand and disappearing inside without another word.

I then turned all my attention to Sean.

He was big and intimidating just like his father, but with him holding his daughter while she slept and drooled down the back of his motorcycle vest—or cut I was told earlier by my daughter—he didn't seem as threatening.

It was with Steel's words bouncing around in my brain that I got the courage to approach.

Today I was using my cane, and I moved a little slower than I would've liked, because before I'd even gotten halfway there, he was on the move again.

"Hey, Sean!"

Sean turned, saw me, and then furrowed his brows.

Sean knew me because he'd denied me a job about a month and a half ago.

He almost looked worried as I approached.

"Yeah?"

I could tell he still felt poorly for not passing me a couple of months ago when I'd gone to retest to continue working PRN—or as needed—with the local ambulance service.

Yet, I knew it wasn't his fault.

I knew it, he knew it, but he still felt bad.

Which then, in turn, caused me to feel bad.

"I'm not here to say anything about you not allowing me to keep my job," I blurted.

He looked relieved to hear that.

"I'm here to ask you if you knew that your father worked without a bullet proof vest on."

His head tilted.

"What?"

I could tell I'd surprised him with my words.

I nodded. "He told me today that he doesn't work with a ballistic vest because the rest of his officers need to be outfitted first…and I was just wondering…last year y'all had that fundraiser for the sheriff's department to get them. You should get them for your dad's department."

Sean's mouth fell open, then he frowned.

"Honey…"

I looked up to see a woman walking toward us, a small smile on her face as she scratched her chin.

She was sizing me up as she approached.

"Hi." I smiled, then waved. "Bye."

Then I turned to walk away.

Women made me nervous.

Really nervous.

I was never really good at making friends, and the fact that the only one I did make really good friends with stole my husband, really made it hard for me to find any common ground with the female population.

I was two steps from the door when I heard him call my name.

I turned and looked at him from across the parking lot.

"Yeah?"

"Thanks for the info. I'll get my dad the vest."

I gave him a thumb up, eerily happy that he'd make sure that his father was safe.

I wish I could do the same, but I just couldn't afford it.

There were days we had to have peanut butter and jelly sandwiches because I couldn't afford to buy groceries for the next four days.

A seven-hundred-dollar vest would buy me groceries for seven weeks, if not more.

"Thank you."

Then I had my hand on the door, about to go inside.

"For what it's worth, I really wanted to pass you," Sean called. "I would have had Arnie not been a dick and told me not to let my soft heart get in the way of our company policy."

I shrugged.

It still hurt, but it was what it was.

I couldn't do anything about it now.

And that's when I found my daughter standing there holding the door open. Listening to what was being said.

"They're ready for us," Conleigh said.

It was when we were in the exam room that she finally spoke.

"He didn't pass you because of your legs?"

I nodded. "He couldn't. I couldn't pass the physical."

"Isn't that discrimination?"

"Not really, no. I couldn't do the job that was demanded of me. I wasn't able to pick up the stretcher without toppling over on my ass. Not much I could do about it," I said, still feeling the humiliation of not being able to do a job that I would've done just fine a year and a half ago.

Conleigh grunted in reply.

I guess she doesn't agree.

CHAPTER 8

Don't be ashamed of who you are. That's your parent's job.
-Fact of Life

Winnie

It was four days later when a hurricane rocked our state. One the likes of which we'd never seen before in the history of the United States.

Everyone was scared.

Even us, and we were nowhere close to the coastline where the majority of the devastation was set to take place.

We'd watched the impending hurricane on the news, and when it finally hit that morning, the coastline of Alabama was hit hard with over thirty inches of rain in ten hours.

It was, quite possibly, the most devastating thing in the world to watch.

The news people were standing outside in the midst of a category five hurricane, and they had to hold on to a chain link fence to keep from being blown away.

Behind them was what used to be a mall parking lot but was now completely submerged. Not even the few stray cars in the parking lot could be seen any longer.

They'd just finished showing a time lapse video of the devastation when I got a call.

"Hello?"

"Winnie, this is Bob."

I smiled. "Hi, Bob. How are you?"

"I'm well. I'm calling to see if you'd be willing to go down to the hurricane affected area and work at our sister hospital for the next week. With the hurricane and the influx of patients, we're sending down about fifty members of our staff to help."

I was about to immediately deny him when he said, "There'll be a ten dollar an hour hazard pay increase, as well as time and a half since you're already at your hours for this week. Free room and board. You'll also be fed, and you'll get bonuses if you do decide to go."

The yes was coming out of my throat before I'd even had the chance to think.

Ten dollars an hour on top of my twelve fifty an hour would make it twenty-two dollars an hour plus time and a half. Hell yes, I was going to do it.

I had Christmas coming up in a few months!

Not to mention that I'd been forced to give Cody up for the next week thanks to the fall break.

Matt had stopped by earlier in the day to beg me to let him have Cody. It was a teacher in-service week, and all the kids were off for the week while the teachers were still expected to go. I hadn't been able to refuse him. Not when I knew my son would love to go.

And then Conleigh had surprised me by asking me if she could go see Matt's parents.

Matt's parents and Conleigh had always been close, and seeing the pleading look in her eyes had left me with a certainty that I needed to loosen my skirt strings a little.

"That's good news." He sounded relieved. "I'm having to look for people that can drive down there. You drive a car, correct?"

I grunted. "Yep. Mine's not going to make it in anything more than about an inch of water."

I looked out my window at the same time to glance at my car, only to find Steel backing his truck up to his camo boat that was always in his garage.

I only ever saw it when he was mowing his grass or was working on the car beside the boat and needed the door up for air.

"There are a lot of duck hunters in the area heading out in their boats. I know that a few of the husbands of some of the nurses are doing it. Let me check with them to see if they have any room in their vehicles for you and get back to you."

Then Bob was gone with a promise to call me back, but I was stuck looking at the man across the street that I somehow knew was about to head down there and do the exact same thing Bob had just described some of the nurses' husbands doing.

I shoved my phone into my pocket and winced when I took my first step.

I'd had therapy today, and the therapist had pushed me harder than she normally did.

A year ago, when I'd had my spinal stroke, I never thought I'd walk again.

Now, here I was walking...without my cane.

I hadn't had to use it at all this week, which had been the deciding factor in my therapist handing out the ass whoopin' she'd given me.

It felt good to have sore muscles, and, as I made my way down the steps with no help there, either, I was smiling.

My smile dropped as soon as I talked to Steel and asked him to take me with him.

***

Steel

"I'm not taking you," I said as I packed up my truck.

"But why?" She pouted, propping both hands on her shapely hips. "Matt has Cody and will have him for the week since it's fall break. Conleigh is spending the time with Matt's parents."

"Because you're…"

"Don't you dare say that I'm a cripple," she snapped. "I'm NOT a cripple."

My eyes narrowed.

"I wasn't going to say that you're a cripple," I informed her. "I was going to say a civilian. You have no experience dealing with water rescue or even boats."

She narrowed her eyes.

"Both of my kids are taken care of," she said. "I'm going because work asked me to and my EMT skills are needed at the hospital. And, honestly, I will be sitting in the truck with you on the drive down there. Nothing else. I swear I won't say a word if you don't want me to. Not to mention all you'll have to do is drop me off at the hospital. Seriously, that's it. I won't be riding around with you. I will be there, safe, helping people that *you* bring in."
I sighed, long and loud.

"Honey…"

"You know," she growled. "Matt used to think that I was useless."

My brows rose.

"He did?"

Winnie was anything *but* useless. Sure, now she was a little slower getting around since she'd had that spinal stroke, but that didn't stop her from doing what she wanted to do. She walked faster with her cane at times than I walked.

I felt every single one of my numerous years catching up to me, especially when it rained.

Like fuckin' today.

Mobile, Gulf Shores, and the rest of the coast had gotten hammered with a hurricane the likes of which I'd never seen before. The huge, category five Hurricane Matt—which still cracked me up that it was the same name as her POS ex-husband— spanned nearly the entire state. It dumped so much fucking rain on us that we'd be feeling its effects for months.

"Yep," she said. "He said I was a useless pile of skin once after my stroke. It was when we were meeting with our lawyers about who would get what." She looked down at where she was standing. "So I started going to the gym. Tried to get my ass back in shape…it's hard, though. I don't know what I'm doing. But at least I can walk now."

I narrowed my eyes.

"He did not. *Please*, tell me he didn't."

She smiled sadly. "He did."

I'd known Matt Holyfield for a long time now. He'd been on the force with us for so long that he was just as much family as my own family—whether I liked him or not. *You couldn't pick family.*

But he'd pulled away from us after he'd met his wife and had his first kid. I had known about Winnie, but I hadn't actually met her until she moved in across the street from me, newly single, with two children in tow.

It just plain surprised me that Matt Holyfield was such a fucking asshole.

"I'll give you a ride, but only to the hospital. Understand?"

She grinned at me, then bounced slightly on her toes as she clapped her hands.

"You won't regret this!" she breathed.

That was a lie.

I was already regretting it.

Having her this near to me, that smile aimed my way, was doing things to my heart.

I didn't want to feel like this about her.

I didn't want to deal with another woman with a shit ton of problems.

And I wasn't saying that Winnie was a problem, just that she had a lot of baggage that I wasn't sure that I could take on.

Not at this point in my life, anyway.

I was well past the age that I should be thinking with my dick.

I would not, under any circumstances, touch one single hair on Winnie's pretty little head. No matter how much I may want to.

All I had to do to cement that fact was think about my exes. Tracy. Lizzibeth. Lila. Terrel. Kay.

All of them I'd given tiny pieces of my heart and every last one of them had broken what little I'd trusted them with.

I had a feeling that if Winnie got anything from me, she would likely hold onto it and never let go.

And I'd have to break it off because I wasn't willing to let her get too close. Not to mention it was highly unlikely she'd want an old man like me for the rest of her life. She'd want things that I just couldn't give her.

Not with what I had on my plate.

Something that I would have to deal with when I got home.

But, the farther and farther we drove together, the more I realized that it might already be too late.

She was under my skin, and I didn't know what to do about it.

Lani Lynn Vale

CHAPTER 9

Sorry I didn't answer your call. I don't really use my cell phone for that.
-Winnie to Steel

Winnie

After checking once more on my children, I put my phone in my pocket and walked into the hospital with my name badge clipped to my scrub pants and Steel at my back.

He was directly behind me mostly because the halls of the hospital were jam packed with people. The halls had been turned into makeshift hospital wards. People were literally in every single inch of available space.

Some guy flew out from behind one of the hastily put together paper partitions and nearly knocked me over.

Steel had me before I so much as stumbled when the man nearly took me out.

"Sorry, sorry," the man, obviously a harried nurse, apologized.

Then he saw my name badge and grinned. "Hi! My name is Tex!"

I blinked. "Hi, Tex."

"Who are you?"

His eyes went from mine to Steel's, and then back again. "Yum."

I started to grin as I said, "I'm here to meet up with the hospital staffer who is doing the emergency staff orientations. Do you happen to know where I should be going?"

Tex snapped his fingers.

"Oh!" Tex said. "That's me! That's so me! I'm here intercepting people to point them in the right direction." He leveled me with a look. "This is a fucking nightmare, by the way. Oh, I'm also not supposed to curse, so we'll just fucking overlook that, okay?"

My lips twitched, and I felt Steel's hand tighten on my hip.

I looked at him over my shoulder.

His beard was dotted with raindrops, and I wanted to lick them off.

I turned back around and sighed.

"So, what do you want me to do, and where can I put my stuff?"

Tex's smile was wide.

"You can put it in the breakroom, but honestly, we really don't have anywhere for you to put anything. Just remember what hours you work and write them down. Send them in when you leave to the email address that we sent out to all the volunteers. Make sure you specify what you do. Now, where I want you is more of a tough question. You're a paramedic?"

He eyed my name badge. "Yes, sir."

Tex's grin was wide. "Not sir. I prefer just Tex. I'm a California guy. We don't say sir and ma'am there. Now, you have your own escort?"

I looked over my shoulder at Steel again.

"Well," I turned back around, trying to ignore the way Tex wouldn't take his eyes off of Steel. "He's a cop and is here because he's helping with search and rescue..."

"What would help tremendously is for a person to be out in the field triaging these patients, directing them to where they need to be." He looked at the man at my back. Steel didn't say a word. "Could you take her? You're going to be in the rescue epi-center anyway. It would work. You could tell the responders whether any of the patients actually need to go to the hospital. And if they don't, then you can direct them to a shelter where they can be checked out there. Would that be okay?"

Would spending more time with Steel be okay? *Hell yes!*

Did Steel want me to be spending more time with him? *Hell no.*

I could tell that he was on edge. Something was bothering him, and I didn't know what.

"I don't know..." I hedged.

Just then, a fight broke out behind Steel's back between a mother of a child on one side of the hallway, and the patient in the bed directly across from them.

"No!" one woman screamed. "I will not allow you to be seen in front of my son. You cut us off on the way into the parking lot. My son has a broken arm."

"I have a fucking broken leg!" the man countered.

Then he emphasized his anger by picking up the IV pole and launching it.

Steel was there before the pole could make contact with the woman.

He had it in his hand and was turning to the man who'd thrown the pole. "I realize," Steel said with a deathly silent voice. "That you are hurting. I realize that you're scared, but you're arguing with a woman over a child. You're packed in here like sardines, so unless you want to be tossed out on your ass, I suggest you stop actin' like a dumbass and control yourself. Capiche?"

The man nodded once, and Steel placed the IV pole back where it was before turning to the woman.

"Your son may have a broken arm, but this man has a goddamn bone sticking out of his leg."

The woman's eyes widened.

"That's a medical emergency."

The woman didn't say anything.

"Stay away from him. Wait your turn."

Then he turned back to me.

His face was hard and unyielding.

"You're coming with me," he said through clenched teeth. "This place is a disaster. There's no way in hell you'd be able to protect yourself in all of this. If he lets you come with me, and you still get paid, I think you should do it."

I licked my lips, then turned back to where Tex was standing in the middle of the cluttered hallway, eyes wide. "That's fine with me. I'm going to give you my number, though, so we can coordinate, okay?"

And that was how I found myself going along with Steel.

Let's just say he wasn't very happy about it.

***

An hour later, and we found ourselves in the middle of a partially flooded parking lot after spending hours trying to get into downtown. The roads were terrible. Most of them were unpassable.

There was so much debris, and crap in the road that the ones that weren't blocked by water were *still* nearly impossible to utilize.

And this parking lot was one of the better parking lots, according to the man who was directly in front of me, talking strategy with Steel.

"You're one of the first ten boats here in this area, so we'd like to get you out on the water as soon as we can. We're always going to have someone staying behind since the water is still rising. If it gets too close to your truck, we'll have someone move it."

Steel nodded. "Fine with me. How are they getting the boats into the water?"

"Some are just backing them up there," he pointed to the parking lot's entrance that almost descended straight into the water like a boat ramp would.

Only, it wasn't a boat ramp. It was really one of those god-awful driveways that you'd normally scrape the bottom of your car on as you were pulling into it.

"Sounds fine…" he looked over to me. "You know how to drive a boat?"

I shook my head. "Negative."

His lips twitched.

That 'negative' had come straight from his mouth every time I'd asked to stop on the way down here.

The one and only time he'd deigned to stop was when I told him I was going to pee on his leather seats if he didn't find me accommodations pronto.

And I was fairly sure he hadn't even gotten out of the truck to pee at all our entire trip.

In fact, I was eyeing the waders he'd slipped on as we'd gotten out of the truck and wondered if he'd gone at all since we'd left. Maybe he had a catheter placed, who knew?

"You got somewhere she can stay?" Steel suddenly asked. "They told her to go to the command tent. That this one?"

The man nodded and then gestured for us to follow.

We did, and I tried not to look down at the disgusting water.

At least I'd brought boots—at Steel's urging.

They were cute, pink, and neoprene. I'd spent about eighty-five dollars on them the week before I'd found out about my husband cheating on me. I'd also bought the kids a pair—which had been the last big purchase for them that I'd been able to make since.

"Yeah, here's as good as any," the man informed me. "That's what we have set up so far. This is the central hub, so they're bringing everyone here first. If you want, you can set your stuff up in that corner and we'll start funneling them toward you."

And that was how the next four hours went until another paramedic, this one from Texas, came to relieve me.

I'd had to pee for the last hour, and it was the best thing ever to see the beautiful redhead.

"Hi!" she chirped. "I'm Winter. Where do you want me?"

I quickly explained what was going on, and then I bowed out. "I have to pee something fierce. I hope you don't mind, but I'm going to head out and find a bathroom."

Winter gestured with a thumb up. "I'll be here when you get back."

I quickly hurried out of the tent and found the first official person I saw. It was a man in a cowboy hat.

"Excuse me," I said.

The man turned, and I was struck with a feeling deep in my gut.

Holy shit, the man was hot.

Like a Viking. And oh, man. His beard! That cowboy hat! Yum. A Viking cowboy. I never knew I had those kinds of fetishes, but here we were. I had the hots for a biker cop, and now there was this really yummy looking Viking cowboy…who also happened to be a cop.

The shiny badge pinned on his shirt said so.

Texas Ranger.

Rawr.

"Yeah?"

"Do you know where the nearest bathrooms are?"

He studied me for a few short seconds, then nodded.

"Yeah, they're that way." He pointed across the parking lot that we were in.

I grinned. "Thank you, Mr. Texas Ranger."

The Texas Ranger winked. "Griffin."

I held up a thumb.

It didn't matter how hot the guy was. I had to pee, and peeing trumped checking out hot guys…at least at this stage in my life.

I rushed as fast as my legs would allow me to rush in the direction that he'd pointed, and made it about halfway across the parking lot to the Boot Barn front doors when I nearly went down flat on my ass.

A man that was leaning against the glass doors started to chuckle, causing me to look up from my crouch.

I'd been able to save myself from hitting the water, but just barely.

By doing so, I'd had to plant my hands onto the grimy asphalt that was covered in about an inch of water.

I grimaced and stood up, carefully checking out my legs.

I felt fine.

In fact, the entire day, my legs had done exactly what I'd wanted them to do—move.

I had no weakness, which was a miracle in and of itself, and I was able to hold my weight.

I would've fist pumped had the guy not still been watching me.

As I shuffled more carefully to the front doors of Boot Barn, I stayed as far away from the man—who seemed vaguely familiar— standing at the door as I could.

He didn't *look* creepy, really, but he gave off a creepy vibe, which meant that I would stay away from him as much as I could.

I opened the door and felt my heart fall when I saw that there was water inside as well as outside.

"Hi," I said to the man behind the counter. "I need to use the facilities."

The older man smiled.

He was old enough to be my grandfather.

"All the way to the back of the store and to the left. If you're hungry, I have some food out on the counter, too," he said. "Cajun food, jambalaya, red beans and rice. Shrimp. You name it, it's in there. I told my Mimi to cook it all up since it was going to go bad anyway with the freezer being off. You're more than welcome to a cup."

I grinned and gave him a heartfelt smile. "I'll take a look. I can smell it from here. It smells amazing."

The old man winked. "Go on, dear."

I did, stopping first at the bathroom before washing my hands and pulling out my phone.

Me (7:12 PM): Are you back yet?

Me (7:16 PM): I'm gonna grab a cup of this yummy smelling jambalaya for you. I'll have it in the tent with me if you get back before I decide to eat it.

Smiling to myself, I looked around for something to serve the food with and realized there wasn't anything.

I eyed the cups that were standing in a stack next to the metal tins of food and shrugged.

Scooping it up in the cup, I juggled both cups and made my way out into the main room again.

This time the creepy man was there talking to the older man.

My stomach clenched as I made my way past the racks of clothes to the front doors.

I smiled at the old man whose eyes were on me.

I intentionally kept my gaze from skittering to the creepy dude.

"Thank you so much for the food. It's amazing."

The old man nodded and waited until I was nearly out of the door before returning his gaze back to the man in front of him.

"Time to go, son," I heard as the door closed fully behind me.

I shivered as I made my way back to the parking lot.

I'd just decided that I would need to wear some better socks in the morning with the boots I was wearing—wondering if Steel had any that he'd let me borrow—when I heard water sloshing behind me.

My stomach started to roil.

I hastened my steps, coming to the conclusion that I shouldn't have come all the way over here in the dark, alone, without an escort. That was rather stupid, and I knew better.

When I was younger, a few weeks shy of nineteen, and walking home from school with Conleigh, I'd had a similar experience.

I'd gotten off shift and had immediately walked over to pick my daughter up from the campus daycare. It was nearly six in the evening, and it being the first or second day after daylight savings time ended, I'd forgotten how dark it got so early.

I'd walked with Conleigh as fast as I could, and had managed to make it three quarters of the way home before realizing that we were being followed.

The man doing the following had been slick. I hadn't even heard or seen him until we were turning the street to our apartment complex.

Instead of going inside my own apartment and leading him to the front door of where I stayed alone with my young child, I went into the laundry mat where quite a few of the young residents had been doing their clothes at the time.

I'd swallowed my heart when I'd arrived inside to find the man standing there watching me.

Two days after the incident, I'd found out that the same man had raped another young mom on a walk home much the same as I had been. I'd been crucial in identifying him during the investigation, and he'd gone to jail for ten years.

Shivering at the thought of him getting out soon, I chanced a look behind me to see that no one was there any longer.

Then I looked forward and stopped.

The reason he wasn't behind me any longer was because he was now in front of me.

What the fuck?

I froze a few inches away from a useless light pole that was about eighty yards away from the command tent and stared, heart in my throat.

"I'm sure you don't remember me…"

I shook my head. "No."

He laughed then. "Funny, because you're all I've been able to think about for a very long time."

I didn't know what to say to that.

I didn't know the man standing in front of me. But then again, the only part of him that I could see was a silhouette from the lights around the command tent at his back.

My stomach was churning.

When I'd gone through that incident with that rapist all those years ago, I'd made a promise to myself that I wouldn't ever put myself into a situation similar to that ever again.

Yet, I'd done it.

Stupid, stupid, stupid.

"I don't know who you are," I admitted. "I'm sorry."

He may seem vaguely familiar, but I couldn't place him at all.

"I guess you wouldn't know this face," the man continued. "Not since it's been put through the ringer these last few years."

I opened my mouth to say something but couldn't find the words.

The more he spoke, the more he became familiar to me, yet I couldn't quite place why.

"Well, I have to be getting back to work," I gestured, moving slightly to the side to try to avoid him.

He stepped with me.

Fear shot down my throat as I tried to calm my breathing.

"I'm not done…"

"Yes," a cruel voice replied behind the man. "You are."

Steel.

Everything inside of me loosened.

I was okay. I was going to be okay.

I looked over the man's shoulder to see not just Steel standing there, but the man with the cowboy hat, too. The Texas Ranger.

While the Texas Ranger wasn't paying attention to me, but instead the man, I hurried around him and bee-lined straight for Steel.

Steel caught my wrist the moment I made it to him and practically shoved me behind him.

The move jostled the food in my hands, and I suddenly realized that throughout the encounter I'd managed to hang onto it and not drop it.

And that, right there, was the telltale sign of just how comfortable I was with Steel. I knew, from the bottom of my heart, that he would protect me. If he was there, nothing, and I do mean absolutely nothing, would happen to me.

He'd protect me to his last dying breath if he had to.

I chanced a look up at the man at Steel's side, and my belly tightened. He didn't look too happy, either.

"Who are you?" Steel rumbled.

I pressed against Steel's back almost automatically. Then thought better of it.

Before I could pull away from him, though, he reached around and placed his hand on my thigh, right under my butt, and stilled me.

The two cups of still steaming hot food were now pressed against his back—which I just now realized he wasn't wearing a rain slicker any longer—and he had to feel it. Yet he held firm as he spoke to the man that had downright terrified me. His hand never strayed up or down, but the position his hand was in was almost intimate.

Other things inside of me started to throb.

I licked my lips, then placed my forehead against the soft material of his t-shirt, directly in the middle of his shoulder blades.

Then I inhaled and forgot what I was doing.

He smelled so good.

Laundry detergent—Tide, the same as mine—a spicy smell that was likely his deodorant, and sweat.

Nothing more, nothing less.

Yet, it did things to me inside that I hadn't felt in quite a long time—not even with my husband.

Matt, after a while, had always felt like a job for me. Something I had to do to keep him interested—which obviously hadn't worked, so who was I kidding?

But just standing there, pressed against Steel's body while he spoke to a man in front of him, I realized what I was missing with Matt after a while.

The intense attraction.

This feelings that I had for Steel? They had the potential to be overwhelming.

Hell, it was damn near at that point already, and I'd only just realized my desire for him over a few weeks.

None of those times that I spent with him, though, were anything I could quite point my finger at as to why I was feeling this for him.

There had been no overt advances on his part, and hell, sometimes I wasn't even sure he liked me.

Yet, the longer he stayed there, his hand on the curve of my ass, the more I realized that the attraction to him was only getting stronger and stronger.

The man at Steel's side shifted, and I heard him start to speak.

"Civilians are being moved out by bus to a different location," the Texas Ranger, Griffin, explained. "The next bus out, you're on it."

"I'm a volunteer," he argued.

"You're not a volunteer," Griffin countered. "You've been standing outside the tent all day, and at first I thought it was because someone you knew was here, but there's not. You're alone, and you haven't done a damn thing to help all day. The next bus that leaves, you're on it."

The bus under discussion pulled up as if Griffin had called it.

They were using the city buses to haul the people out, taking them to a temporary holding facility. Once they made room at the shelter, they'd be moved from the temporary holding facility to the newest shelter.

"I'm here with my sister."

"Who's your sister?" Steel questioned.

The man opened his mouth, then closed it.

"Get on the bus now," Steel growled.

The man narrowed his eyes, his gaze scanning from the tips of Steel's toes to the top of his head. Then took note of the arm that he had around my ass and the eyes that I now had aimed at him.

Then smiled.

"Yes, sir."

Then he walked to the bus and got on it, all the while whistling an upbeat tune.

"Fucker has been creeping me out all damn day," Griffin growled.

Suddenly Steel turned, and I had to raise the cups up high in the air to keep him from knocking them to the floor with the suddenness of his movements.

"Whoa," I said, swaying slightly.

He caught me around the hip and his hands came to a rest on my sides, which were now exposed due to me lifting my arms in the air.

He squeezed lightly, making sure I was steady, and then let me go.

His eyes, though…those eyes of his said he'd rather do anything *but* let me go.

But the look was gone in a blink of his eyes, and his careful expression was back on my face.

"Are you okay?"

I felt his concern in the pit of my belly, and I wanted nothing more than to launch myself into his arms.

I was scared.

That man…he brought up terrible memories.

I was so lost in my own mind, my hands still in the air, that I didn't realize when Steel's face turned from assessing to concerned.

The cups were removed from my hands, and Steel handed them over to Griffin.

"Winnie?"

He took my arms and brought them down, curling one hand around both of mine with room to spare.

I blinked, coming back to myself, and said, "Yeah?"

That's when I realized he'd flattened both of my hands to the hard plane of his chest.

Jesus Christ.

Now my mind was lost for an altogether different reason.

I knew that Steel was older. Hell, it was hard to miss the silvering gray hair, and the way his beard was more gray than brown at this point.

But I hadn't really realized how in shape he was—now I knew differently. Steel was just that…steel.

His muscular chest didn't have an ounce of fat on it.

I wondered what it looked like when he had his shirt off…

"Winnie."

The hard, even tone of Steel's voice had me blinking. "I'm sorry, what?"

"Are you okay?"

I nodded once, my fingertips itching to run along his chest.

"Are you sure?"

I swallowed, then nodded. "When I was nineteen, I had a close call. That guy reminded me of it is all."

"A close call."

I nodded.

"What kind of close call?"

"The kind where someone followed me and Conleigh home, but he didn't actually get anything accomplished before I ducked into the laundry room of our apartment complex. The next day, the same thing happened to another girl, only she wasn't as lucky as me."

His eyes studied my face.

"What was his name?"

My stomach started to churn despite having Steel right there.

Every time I thought about what could've happened to me—to Conleigh because he hadn't just stopped at women—my belly started to protest.

"Anderson Munnick," I answered. "He was a…"

"A serial rapist that they could only pin one rape on," Griffin answered. "You remember that case that rolled through Texas a few years back? Those ones that we called every single chief of police in the state of Alabama to warn?"

Steel's hand tightened on my wrist.

"You testified."

I nodded. "I did."

His eyes warmed. "Good girl."

A moment passed in between us where we stared at each other. His praise made me feel light and airy, and I wanted to bury my face in between his two perfect pecs.

"What is this?" Griffin suddenly asked.

I looked over at him studying the contents of the cup.

"Jambalaya," I answered. "The man up there had his wife cook the contents of their freezer since their power was out and the meat was going to spoil. She cooked jambalaya, stew, and about ten different kinds of meat."

Griffin grunted. "Smells fucking divine."

"You can have it," I offered, then turned to the man still holding my hands to his chest. "I brought you one, Steel."

"Thanks," he said, finally realizing that he was still holding me and letting go. "Are you sure you don't want it?"

I nodded. "My appetite is gone."

Steel studied me for a few more seconds before he nodded.

"They're likely about to move this to higher ground," Steel suddenly said. "The levees that are holding back the lake in town are about to break. That means when it does, this parking lot is going to be underwater. Are you ready?"

Wide-eyed, I nodded.

"But what about everyone else in the tent?"

I looked over my shoulder at the tent and noticed that there weren't nearly as many people around as there had been when I'd first left for the bathroom.

"They're shipping out. The new central evac point will be about a mile and a half up the road. Higher ground," Griffin muttered, taking a cautious bite of his food.

Then he moaned.

"Oh my God. This shit is the bomb."

He brought the cup of food up to his lips and started to drink it like one would when they chugged a beer.

I started to laugh, then shook my head and turned my gaze back to the man that was still studying me.

"I'm ready when you are."

He nodded once. "Right."

Then we spent the rest of the night and way into the early hours of the morning helping.

An hour after six in the morning, we finally hit Steel's truck.

"I'm dying," I moaned, shucking my wet boots and setting them carefully into the floorboard of the backseat.

Steel grunted. "Fucking rain. If I never see another goddamn drop of it again it'll be too soon."

Another raindrop hit the windshield then, causing me to laugh.

"You were saying?"

He sighed.

"These pants are fucking wet as fuck."

He'd taken his waders off before he'd gotten into the truck, but at some point during the night, Steel had sunk into the water past his waders as he tried to rescue an elderly woman from her car.

He'd spent the rest of the night wet, but he hadn't once complained.

Until now.

"Take them off," I suggested. "I'll close my delicate eyes."

He scoffed as he reached for the waistband of his jeans. "They're coming off whether I had your permission or not."

My heart rate skyrocketed as I slapped my hands over my eyes.

I heard the clink of his buckle and the slide of his zipper before he cursed while he shoved the wet pants down his legs.

"Shit," he cursed. "Can you reach my bag?"

Could I reach his bag?

"Where is it?" I questioned, still keeping my hands over my eyes even though I wanted to do nothing but open my eyes and stare at him.

He had to be naked at this point. *Had to.*

"It's behind the back seat. You'll have to crawl back there and reach behind the seat for it.

I carefully started to crawl back there without opening my eyes.

"You *so* owe me," I informed him.

He started to chuckle.

"Duly noted."

And that, ladies and gentlemen, was how I got my first good look at the man who was, indeed, sitting in his seat buck naked.

I'd had to open my eyes to see what I was doing, and I'd turned only to get an eye full of naked Steel.

Wet, naked Steel.

Wet, naked Steel who was looking at me in his rear-view mirror.

Shit!

"Sorry!" I squeaked. "I forgot!"

He started to laugh. "I'll take my peek at you when you change out of *your* wet clothes."

And, ten minutes later when we were both dry, I wondered if he did indeed peek.

The expression on his face was void of anything telling, however.

Leaving me only to guess.

My guess is that he did look but that might only be my hopes and dreams talking.

CHAPTER 10

Some days I eat salads and go to the gym. Other days I eat three
pounds of bacon and drink a dozen beers. I call it balance.
-Steel to Winnie

Winnie

Curiosity killed the cat.

In this instance, it almost killed Winnie.

Me.

Shit!

"What are you reading?"

I slapped my laptop closed and smiled guiltily.

"Nothing."

He grunted something in reply and went to his bag for a new pair
of underwear and a dry pair of jeans.

"Tomorrow I'm gonna need my flannel back!" he said. "It's the
only thing dry I have left! Plus, I'm an old man. I need to stay
warm."

I grimaced and looked down at my attire.

I was wearing his flannel shirt, but only because my own shirts just weren't cutting it.

With the hurricane came a cool front, and that cool front was chilly to the point that I needed more clothes than I'd brought.

We'd tried to stop and pick up a sweatshirt from a drug store, but apparently along with the food on the shelves, everyone had bought all the sweatshirts they had in stock as well.

"You're so full of shit. You're not that old." I headed to the bathroom door.

"I'm old."

"Not old enough that it matters."

He turned and gave me a long look that felt like he'd stripped me bare.

"I'm old enough to be your father."

I laughed. "You're not. But even if you were, why would that matter?"

"It matters because I'm old, and you're young. You're in the prime of your life, while I have an adult son that could be your brother. It's just...odd." He finally settled on.

I felt my heart beating faster. "Yes...but the heart wants what the heart wants."

He looked away.

"And, just sayin', but I have a sixteen-year-old."

"But you also have a five-year-old." He pointed out. "And an ex-husband that is a part of his life. I've done my civic duty...and I'm honestly over the ex game. Trust me when I say, I'm too old for you. Too jaded. Too set in my ways."

I grunted but didn't call him on his bullshit.

"Just…I need my shirt, okay?"

I realized that the matter was closed, and we wouldn't be discussing it anymore…at least tonight.

Okay, then.

"Okay," I called. "But I can wear it right now?"

He slammed the door closed.

"Yeah," he yelled through the door. "Do you want me to leave the shower on for you?"

I moaned. "No. I already took one while you were getting dinner."

"Okay."

Then the shower turned on and I guiltily opened my laptop once again.

The webpage I had up was a blog that I loved to follow.

It was composed of two mothers around my age, both of whom were hilariously funny.

Today's topic of conversation was blow jobs.

I'd never been good at blow jobs, and honestly, I didn't have to be. Why? Because Matt didn't like them.

Yes, I know. It was weird. What guy didn't like blow jobs?

I'd tried to give Matt a blow job once and only once, and he'd started to freak out because my mouth was too close to him.

See, Matt had a fear of mouths.

Yes, you heard that correct.

Mouths.

He was grossed out watching me brush my teeth. He didn't like kissing me. (And, from what I'd heard, he didn't mind kissing Slut-Bag Angelina, which chafed.) He abhorred going to the dentist because someone was going to be doing stuff in his mouth, and the icing on the cake was his incessant need to get away from me—or our kids—if it even looked like they were going to open their mouths near him.

Dear God, there was this one time that Matt had been holding Cody when he yawned near his face. I still remember it like it was yesterday instead of years ago.

He'd been sitting on the couch, Cody—who'd only been a few months old at the time—resting on his chest. Cody had lifted his head, brought his face almost directly into Matt's, and then yawned.

Yawned.

That was all he'd done.

And it was like Cody had projectile vomited down his throat instead of just doing a normal bodily function.

He'd practically thrown Cody across the couch.

I still remember the bounce he'd done before almost landing on the floor.

Had Conleigh not been there, catching him before he could continue his roll, he'd have landed face first on the corner of the coffee table.

Fucking Matt.

I'd never, not once, had the pleasure of giving a blow job.

Yet, I wanted to give one.

I wanted to give one to Steel.

Jesus Christ, did I want to give him one.

The man turned me on in ways that I had no clue were my turn-ons, yet here I was, wondering what it would feel like to give the man a blow job.

My curiosity got the better of me as I googled more tips—which they'd said they'd done as a comparison—and then I got lost in the World Wide Web.

My first stop had been *Cosmopolitan!*

My second had been some random Joe-Blow (literally, that was the name of the website) blog that gave the men's top ten best blow job tips—according to men.

1. Maintain eye contact.

2. Tie your hair back, it shows your dedication.

3. Allow him to put his hand in your hair and control the movements.

That, I could do! In fact, the idea of Steel putting his hands in my hair and controlling all of the movement was downright arousing.

4. Use your hand as well as your mouth. Twist it side to side lightly as you pump and suck him.

Okay, pump, suck and twist. Check!

5. Don't use your teeth. Ever.

I shivered at the thought. That would suck, accidentally biting Steel's dick. He'd probably never let me near him again and kick me straight the hell out of his bed. Though, I had to get in his bed first…

6. Drop down so he's standing and you're kneeling. There's nothing more arousing than watching a woman get on her knees.

That thought made me shiver. Would Steel like me on my knees?

I sure the hell hoped so. I'd love to get on my knees for him.

Then again, I was doing good with my rehab…he still might have to help me back up.

I winced. Maybe I should just get on the bed between his splayed thighs…yes, that was how I'd do it.

7. Suck his balls.

Suck his balls? How the hell did I put those in my mouth? There wasn't enough room!

8. Go slow. It's not a race.

9. Swallow.

Well, that was self-explanatory. But I didn't know if I *could* swallow. I'd try, but what if I gagged?

10. We like it when you gag.

Did they? What if I accidentally threw up? That would completely ruin the mood.

"What are you doing?"

I squeaked and jumped as Steel came out of the bathroom.

After our first night together, he hadn't bothered to be modest around me in the least.

If we weren't working, I quickly realized, Steel would rather be shirtless.

I quickly shut my laptop and smiled.

"Reading," I lied.

Well, I guess technically it wasn't a lie. I was reading. What I wasn't doing was reading a book.

I flushed.

"Hmmmm," he said. "You ready for bed?"

I nodded.

We were in a hotel room in the outskirts of whatever city we were in. I couldn't remember which one it was at this point seeing as we'd been to so freakin' many over the last two days.

We were lucky to find a hotel room, to be honest. Yesterday we'd slept in Steel's truck in a convoy of other rescuers, on the side of the road.

I'd slept like a freakin' baby.

"Yep!" I lied.

I wasn't ready for bed. Not even a little bit.

But tomorrow was going to be another long, exhausting day. Then we had to drive home because Steel—as well as I—had to return to work.

Steel moved around the room turning off lights as I snuggled deeper under my blankets.

I shivered, wondering again why it was so cold in here.

The air wouldn't turn off. We'd tried. Multiple times.

And, sadly, it wasn't one of those window units where you could just unplug it. Nope, not this hotel. It was fancy—and by fancy, I mean four hundred dollars a night fancy.

Yes, I'd almost swallowed my tongue at hearing that price come out of the concierge's mouth.

However, they'd expressly informed us that they were having problems with their air conditioning systems—not that they would be comping the room for us or even reducing the price because of it, mind you.

Luckily, we were informed, that we got one of the rooms with air. Apparently, about half the hotel didn't have it due to surges in power during the storm.

However, what air the other half of the hotel wasn't getting, we were.

Meaning it was a chilly fifty degrees up in this bitch.

"You want my blanket?"

I shook my head. "No."

Also, along with the fact that it was cold, there weren't any extra blankets to be had. With the hotel being so close to the area of disaster, people had flooded the hotel with their families. In some rooms, I'd noticed how there were as many as ten people in it. Obviously, they'd gotten the extra blankets.

This also meant that we were left with what was on the bed only.

A single white sheet, a small waffle-pleated blanket, and two pillows per queen bed.

Two.

My bag had dropped out of the truck earlier into a puddle of muddy water, and because of that, I was wearing a pair of my panties and one of Steel's shirts...and nothing else.

All of my other belongings were now being washed and dried— promised to be returned by morning—by the hotels extremely high-priced laundry service department.

"Are you sure?" He pushed.

"I'm fine."

I wasn't fine, but I sure as hell wasn't going to take Steel's blanket when it was fifty fucking degrees in here.

Dammit.

Without argument, he turned off the light.

Then I heard him stripping his pants off, the belt clinking against the ground as he dropped them, and then the bed squeaking as he climbed under the covers.

I licked my lips, wondering if I'd ever work up the courage to touch the man.

I've seen the appreciative looks he'd send me, but since he apparently thought I still needed time, he was giving me the space that he must have thought I needed.

Space that I didn't need.

Not at all.

Not anymore, anyway.

Not after knowing Steel Cross for the time that I had.

I wanted him.

I liked how he took care of my kids. I liked how he took care of me—even when he tried to act inconspicuous as he did. And I liked him.

A lot.

He made me laugh. He humored me when I did things I probably shouldn't want to do—like this trip with him to the hurricane-affected area for example. He also took care of me even when I didn't think I needed to be taken care of.

He was an all-around great guy.

But he also had a streak of bad boy in him.

He was a president of a motorcycle club. He was brash, hard, and unforgiving.

I'd watched him take down a criminal—right in the middle of our street—who had been trying to break into my car.

Seriously, I loved the good guy part of Steel Cross, I truly did. But I needed the bad boy in him. I needed him with the power of a thousand suns.

In my vagina.

Soon.

I just had to find a way to let him know that.

And, as my eyes closed, and I thought about anything but the freezing temperature of the room around me, I realized that I would have to flat out tell him that I wanted him. Otherwise, he wouldn't make the move.

He'd actually said he'd have dated me in a different lifetime, before our lives had gotten so complicated, on our drive down.

Maybe I needed to show him that we didn't have to make it more complicated than it already was.

Maybe we should uncomplicate things.

Shivering even harder than I already was at that thought, I closed my eyes and felt my eyes grow heavy.

I didn't fully drop off into sleep.

Couldn't. Not with my teeth clattering together every couple of seconds, and chills racing over my body making the bed springs underneath me squeak.

My dreams, however, were beautiful.

I closed my eyes and drifted, thinking of him.

Somehow, I found myself warm despite my knowing I shouldn't be.

I didn't care how. Didn't honestly care why. I just cared that I was deliciously warm, and was finally able to get to sleep.

***

Hours later, my eyes opened.

A sound had woken me...what had it been?

Another sound, a bump from the room toward my head, sounded again.

The bed.

A bed was hitting the wall that our bed was on.

Our bed?

That's when I noticed that I was no longer alone in my bed.

I had a distinctly male body practically underneath me.

My leg was thrown over one strong thigh. My head was resting on the strong, slightly hairy chest, with a strong heartbeat beneath. My panty-clad pussy was pressed up against a distinctly male hip. One of my arms was crossed over a very hard belly, and finally, a strong fist was tangled in my unruly hair.

I was in Steel's bed. Laying half on top of Steel's very hard body with my own. Holy *shit*.

My knee was about halfway across his hips, resting lightly just above where the waistband of his underwear rested.

I moved my calf slightly to the right, bringing my foot to rest directly between his thighs on the bed. It also meant that my calf was now pressing against his dick.

His dick that was currently soft, yet still hard...if that made any sense at all.

I could feel it there, and all of a sudden, I wished I had nerve endings in my calf like I did in my fingers.

I tried to feel his cock. Tried to imagine what it looked like.

And then I shifted.

I couldn't help it.

I brought my leg farther down until it—his cock—rested against the side of it.

Then, ever so slowly, I moved my hand as if I was still asleep. It came to a rest right above his boxer briefs and stilled.

Two fingers were resting on the band itself, and the other three were resting on his skin. Skin that was covered in a soft trail of hair that led the way to where I most wanted my fingers.

Shit, shit, shit.

The heat between my legs grew, and suddenly I could feel myself getting wetter, something I'd never before accomplished outside of when I was reading a really good smutty book.

Oh God.

This was torture.

My fingers itched to move.

I wanted them somewhere else so bad that they actually twitched.

My middle finger slipped under the waistband and came to a halt.

Everything inside of me screamed.

I hadn't meant to do that, yet I couldn't move them again.

What if he woke up? He was going to wake up. He'd have to wake up.

Oh God.

I squirmed inwardly, wanting to grind myself against him at the same time that I also wanted to shove my hands down his pants the rest of the way.

The bed hit the wall again and then again.

That's when I felt Steel stiffen.

Both in body and in cock.

I was unsure how our position came to be, but I assumed that Steel had either moved me to his bed, or he moved to mine.

I couldn't see any light in the room due to the blackout curtains, so I couldn't even tell where we were in the room.

But I could feel Steel all around me.

His arm tightened slightly around my shoulders and then dropped.

His hand met bare skin, which was when I realized that my shirt had somehow ridden up.

And when I say it rode up, I meant that I could feel my bare breasts against his very hot chest.

Oh, fuck.

Goddammit, I was horny.

I didn't dare move.

Whatever had gotten us into this mess was a Godsend.

That's how I took it, anyway.

I'd needed a way to get closer, and he'd practically given it to me by crawling into bed with me.

I couldn't help that my body was attracted to his, drawn to him like a magnet.

He tried to move away from me slightly, and I did what any sane woman would do in this situation.

I moved, acting like I was still asleep, and practically rolled straight over on top of him.

He didn't move for a long minute.

I didn't, either.

Couldn't, really.

I was sure, any second, he'd roll me off of him. My heart was thundering in my chest, and I could feel his cock—which was definitely getting harder by the second—against my inner thigh.

My breasts were now fully pressed against his chest, and I was right.

He had chest hair. Quite a bit of it, actually.

Saliva filled my mouth, but I didn't dare swallow.

He'd know. I knew it. If I so much as did anything overtly obvious, he'd roll me off and tell me this wasn't a good idea.

So I stayed still.

It was the hardest thing I'd ever done.

His cock, also, never deflated.

In fact, I almost wanted to say it got harder.

It took everything I had not to grind myself against him.

My clit was throbbing, I could feel my wetness saturating my underwear, and I knew that soon, it'd be obvious to not just me but him, too.

His hand came up and he fisted my hair again, tugging it lightly.

I couldn't help it.

I moaned and rubbed myself against him.

He froze again. For long, drawn out seconds, he paused and didn't move. Didn't even breathe.

Then his hand—the one that wasn't fisted in my hair—came down to rest on my ribs.

His thumb came out and swept down, swiping all the way along my outer breast.

My nipples pebbled.

He did it again, and this time I couldn't help but squirm on top of him.

His hand moved down the length of my back to my leg that was resting between his thighs, and he pulled it up until it was resting on the outside of his other thigh.

I moved then, re-centering myself on his body until my breasts were in the middle of his chest, my head tucked up underneath his chin, and my pussy centered directly over his very hard cock.

And that's about the time that the people on the other side of the wall really started to go at it.

It was also when he realized that I was no longer even remotely asleep.

"Awake?"

I swallowed, then nodded.

"Thank fuck."

I grinned and brought my head up, searching blindly in the dark for his mouth.

His beard was the first thing my lips touched, and then his hand was there, guiding my head until I was lips-to-lips with him.

"There," he said against them.

I kissed him then, relishing in the act.

Matt hadn't ever let me do this.

But Steel?

He owned my mouth.

Fucking. Owned. It.

He dragged my mouth to his, took what he wanted and didn't let me go.

Not until I was out of breath and grinding against him in desperation.

But I wanted to do something. I wanted to do it so bad that I actually said what I wanted.

And he didn't argue.

Not even a little bit.

"I want you in my mouth. I want it so bad."

He growled something against my lips, and then he was helping me down between his legs.

The blanket went with me as I crawled, and the fist in my hair stayed as I settled myself and hooked my fingers in the waistband of his underwear.

I pulled them down and then realized with dismay that I wanted to see what I was doing. Really, really bad.

"I want to see," I breathed.

I felt him move underneath me, and then a light lit up the room.

I looked at his cock, suddenly right in front of my face, and my heart dropped.

"What?"

He read the devastation on my face.

"I read about how to give a blow job—but I can't give you one," I told his dick.

His cock jumped.

"Why?"

I could hear the strain in his voice, and I knew instantly that I was going to give him one whether I knew how to do it or not. The huskiness that had overtaken him was downright sexy.

He wanted my mouth on his cock.

"Because you have an uncut dick…" I told him. "I don't know what to do with an uncut dick."

He laughed, and the laugh caused his cock to jump up, tapping my lips.

We both groaned.

"It's the same as cut dicks, honey," he explained with a humor laced, husky voice. "Just a little bit of extra skin."

"What do I do with the extra skin?" I questioned him, touching the tip of his cock that was covered by the extra skin under question.

"Pull it back."

I pushed it with one finger, revealing the head of his cock—his leaking cock—and let it go.

The skin pushed back up, but it didn't go as far this time, stuck right around the crest of his cock head and stayed.

Now his cock head remained in view, and I couldn't help myself. I had to touch his cock with my tongue. *I had to.*

So I did.

I bent down and licked the little bead of come off the tip of his cock.

His entire body stiffened, but he didn't try to grab me. Didn't try to rush me.

"Tell me what else is different about your cock," I ordered.

Steel started to chuckle, and I watched, fascinated, as his cock moved each time a burst of laughter poured from his beautiful lips.

That's when I lost the battle with my curiosity and swirled my tongue around the head of his cock.

He brought my hand up to his cock and wrapped me around him as I did.

I looked up at him and watched him watching me.

"Pull it down like this," he ordered.

I did as instructed, wrapping my hand timidly around his cock.

He tightened his hand and made me fist him like I was holding onto him for dear life.

"I won't break."

No, with the cock he had, I didn't think he would.

It was big, thick and beautiful.

Honestly, I'd seen pictures of uncircumcised cocks on the internet. They looked like aardvarks…or at least the ones I'd looked at had.

This one that Steel was wielding, though? Yeah, no aardvark for him.

His was a pipe. The foreskin had acted like a shield for what lay underneath, but once it was revealed, well…the man wasn't lacking in the cock department.

The tip of his cock was ruddy and there was a healthy drop of fluid coming out of the crown. The actual shaft was riddled with veins, and he had a very juicy one on the underside of his cock that ran the entire length of his penis. So juicy, in fact, that I found myself licking up and down, loving the way it pulsed against my wet tongue.

As a paramedic, veins were my porn.

Steel had some nice ones on his arms. I'd dreamed about giving him an IV. But this one? The one that I was currently running my tongue up and down? Yeah, I was fairly sure that no other would ever displace it from number one.

It would be forever dubbed 'the best vein' in my personal book of vein porn. It would never have its crown taken away.

Not ever.

"Suck me into your mouth already."

I glanced up, remembering about the eye contact, and then sucked just the tip into my mouth.

He about came off the bed.

That's when I started noticing his body.

I'd seen his shirt plastered to his chest, and his pants against his thighs, for days now.

But, seeing him naked and watching me down the length of his body?

Yeah, his penis vein wasn't the only thing that was going to be a reoccurring spankbank memory.

This image? The one where I was looking up the length of his body? Yeah, I'd remember it forever, too.

The way his chest hair gathered on his muscular, defined pectorals, then funneled down his chest in a sort of triangle shape to puddle in a skinny pool along the length of his abs.

Abs.

Plural.

Steel was in his fifties, that I'd been able to ascertain.

I didn't know his exact age, but I knew for a fact that any man would be lucky to have the body that Steel did at his age.

He was goddamn gorgeous.

I also knew that he liked to eat healthy.

After eating with him over the last couple of days, I knew that he got the best thing on the menu, regardless of where we were.

For instance, the day before yesterday we stopped at a gas station. They had typical gas station food. What they didn't have, however, was anything healthy but a basket of fruit in the front of the store, and a turkey sandwich on wheat bread in the cooler next to the fruit.

While I had always gravitated toward foods that were healthy for me due to my marathon training—which I *would* get back to—it was a rare sight to see a man gravitate toward it, too.

And looking at him now in all his glory, it showed.

"Push the skin back and suck me down."

I pulled his skin back with my hand while my mouth went farther down his length.

His abs clenched, and I gagged slightly when his hips lifted involuntarily, causing his cock to hit the back of my throat.

"Sorry, girl." He closed his eyes, likely searching for control.

I looked back down at his cock since he wasn't looking at me any longer, and moaned when I felt a drop of pre-come touch the taste buds on the tip of my tongue.

He tasted good.

A lot better than I was expecting him to.

I sucked him up and down, then let his dick fall from my mouth as I took a good look at his balls.

They were big, but I had faith that I could do this.

Pushing his dick up and sideways, I dropped my mouth farther between his legs and tentatively licked his balls.

He cursed, and suddenly I had two hands in my hair instead of one.

I thought at first that he was going to yank me up, but he held still, the only thing changing was the tighter grip in my hair. Hair that was quickly escaping the hap-hazard bun I'd tied it into before falling asleep.

I could feel some of the wispy pieces of my hair falling against my face, but I didn't care. Not then. Maybe later, when it was all said and done, I'd care that he was tangling it beyond redemption, but now? Now I was too engrossed with the way his body was a live wire waiting for the next shoe to drop.

"Fuckkkk."

I almost grinned, but I didn't want to take my mouth away from the ball that I'd lovingly sucked inside of my mouth.

Reverently, I swirled it around on my tongue, relishing in the way he tensed and shook each time I jacked his cock off and sucked lightly on his ball.

It was as I was shifting over to the other neglected member of his anatomy when he struck.

One second, I was on my knees between his legs, and the next I was on my back with Steel's hulking form towering over me.

I gasped and spread my legs in surprise.

He fell more fully between my hips, and then his cock was pressed against my pussy.

My pussy that was more than ready to take whatever he was willing to give.

His eyes met mine, and I saw resolve there.

We were doing this.

He thought I was too young.

I wasn't.

But he thought I was.

He didn't want to get involved with me. I had two kids, an ex-husband that all of a sudden wanted something to do with me and my kids now that Steel had started hanging around, and that was the last thing he needed.

He had an ex-wife who called every couple of days asking for money. He had an ex-girlfriend who was dead set on getting back together with him. And he had a motorcycle club and a job that demanded the rest of his time.

He didn't have time for me and my kids.

Yet, he'd done okay so far.

He'd let us take a peek into his life, and he'd taken my daughter under his wing.

We were already there.

I was already there.

And now, so was he.

"Steel…"

"Call me Big Papa," he ordered. "Nobody but you calls me Steel."

I grinned and shook my head. "Maybe outside of bed. But I'm definitely not calling you that *in* bed. And, I'll call you that when I feel like it, and not a second before."

"Steel makes me feel old. No one has called me Steel since my parents were alive twenty years ago," he growled.

"You're older, yes." I ran my hands up his chest, then circled them around to his pectorals. My fingers flicked over both of his nipples, causing him to jerk. "But you're sexy."

He smirked.

"I've been watching you since we moved in," I admitted. "I was so freakin' mad at Matt. There was nothing in this world that would make me consider going for another alpha male…then you came around the first time. You were checking your mail. Some kid was driving too fast down the street, and you stepped out in front of him. Then you proceeded to scare the crap out of him. You had on a pair of worn-out jeans that fit your ass perfectly and a tight black t-shirt. But that kid looked at you, scared to death, and hung on your every word. Just like I did, and have done, since."

"Winnie…"

"I'm broken, or at least I thought I was broken. But over the last couple of months, you've shown me exactly what a real man is, and Matt was never one. I know that down to the bottom of my heart. You showed me, and then you helped me get over him. You made me realize that what I had with him wasn't anything compared to what I could have with you."

"I'm not good stock, baby," he said. "My track record is shit…but I can offer you this."

His 'this' was followed by a grind of his hips.

His cock split the lips of my sex, and then he was sliding up and down the length of me in slow, shallow strokes.

I wanted more with him…but I was hesitant.

I didn't want to be disappointed again. I didn't want to find out that he wasn't what I'd made him out to be.

But…the way he was with Conleigh? That was everything to me.

Everything.

I've never once seen Matt act like that with her. He'd been there physically, taken care of some of her basics needs, but he never treated her like a daughter, building a relationship with her and teaching her the ways of the world. He didn't offer to take her fishing or do anything with her one-on-one, and he never got her anything that she didn't actually need.

When she started to slip into one of those moods that all teenage girls got into, Matt would yell at her and tell her to go to her room. Steel talked her through it. Found out what the core of her problem was.

It was the sexiest thing in the world to watch.

He actually cared about my kids.

He didn't just tolerate them.

And that, out of anything he could've done to win me over, was enough to make me love him forever.

"I don't care," I told him. "I want you. I want this. I don't care if you can promise me tomorrow. I don't care if you can't give me forever. I want you now, and that's all I wish to think about."

"In that case, we're doing this."

I would've laughed had he not pulled away from me at the same time as he spoke.

"Where are you going?" I gasped, missing his heat almost instantaneously.

"Condom," he said as he started to push himself off the bed.

I reached for his wrist and yanked him back.

If he hadn't wanted to come, he wouldn't have.

But I could tell his control was nearly gone.

"No condoms," I ordered. "Just you and me."

"Winnie…"

"I'm on birth control. I've been tested, too. Matt…he…well. He cheated, and I had to make sure that he didn't give me anything. I had to be sure. And since I was there, I had them put an IUD in."

I barely got the words out before he was on me.

That control gone.

His cock was at my entrance, and then he was pushing inside of me.

There was no resistance.

No waiting.

No nothing.

All of a sudden, I was just filled. His big body was up against mine, and his chest hair was tickling my nipples as he planted himself to the root and stilled.

My eyes were too busy rolling back in my head to notice the look of pure desire and possession on his face. Because, if I had, I would've known that he was just as deep in this as I was.

I would've known that he was feeling more than he was saying.

But I didn't have any control over my eyes—or the rest of my body—when his cock was inside of me.

His huge, thick, filling-me-to-the-brim dick.

I didn't think I'd ever be the same.

"Oh God," I breathed. "You're so big."

"You're just small."

"No," I shook my head. "You're big. I've had two kids. They sewed me up tighter than tight…but I had you in my mouth. I had your dick against my face. You're big. Trust me on this."

He started to laugh.

I would have, too, but then he pulled out and then thrust back in.

My breasts bounced under my shirt, drawing his eyes.

"Take the shirt off."

I did, taking the shirt off and throwing it down onto the bed.

It landed next to my face, half of it touching my neck.

I didn't take the time to remove it, though, because all of a sudden, he was fucking me so hard that I couldn't breathe.

He was hitting my cervix with each thrust of his cock inside of me, and I couldn't quite make my brain work.

It was as if the pleasure he was pulling from me was short-circuiting my brain.

Then his mouth was headed downward, and my nipple was pulled between those perfect lips. His beard tickled my chest, and I couldn't hold it in any longer. I came. And came. And came.

Implosion.

There were no other words for what happened to me.

His grunt had me gasping for air, and all of a sudden, I felt him coming inside of me.

Bursts of his release filled me up, making me a hundred times slicker than I'd been before, and easing the way for his thrusts.

Then I was holding his heat in my arms.

I couldn't breathe with his entire upper body plastered to mine, but I didn't care.

Not one single bit.

Because Steel fucking Cross was in my arms, and I was as happy as I could fucking be.

***

The next morning, we both woke up at once, but it was me that reached forward for my phone.

I had it in my hand and placed to my ear moments later, thinking the only person that called this early was Conleigh.

Which made me worried almost from the start of the conversation.

"Hello?"

Silence.

"Hello?" I repeated.

"Who is this?"

I pulled the phone away from my face and stared at the screen.

Lizzibeth.

I didn't have a Lizzibeth in my contacts…

"Shit, sorry," I said, putting the phone down on Steel's chest. "That's your phone, not mine."

He started to chuckle. The sound was deep and husky.

"Not a problem," came his just as deep and husky reply.

It was at that instant that everything we'd done the night before came back to me. Everything.

And I wanted it.

Again.

My hand slowly slid down his chest as he picked the phone up to his ear.

"Yeah?"

I shivered and hoped that he'd never direct that particular tone towards me. Ever.

Lani Lynn Vale

CHAPTER 11

Some men dream of being a hero. Others relive it in their nightmares.
-Steel's secret thoughts

Steel

"Yeah?" I answered.

I didn't have to look at the screen to know who it was. Lizzibeth didn't miss a chance to call and rail me in the morning.

"Who was that?"

I looked down at the head that was resting on my chest and grinned.

"That was Winnie. What do you want?"

"Winnie?" she sneered. "Just who the hell is Winnie?"

I didn't know what exactly Winnie was to me, so I chose not to answer.

"Is there a reason you're calling me?"

"You…you…you're already seeing someone else?"

That was about the time that Winnie started to run her hand in circles along the hair on my chest. Her fingers started to graze my nipples with each pass, and, surprisingly, she was making me hard just by that touch alone.

My nipples weren't sensitive…at least I hadn't thought they were.

Now…with her. Apparently, they were.

"Lizzibeth, we've been over for almost a year. And, to be honest, it was a moment of stupidity on my part for marrying you in the first place. I never loved you…I just loved the idea of you."

That's when Winnie started to silently laugh into my chest, her face against the left side of my chest, her mouth inches away from my nipple.

I could feel her hot breath brushing against it, and my cock stiffened even further.

"I cannot believe you," she hissed. "I cannot. I can't."

I refrained from telling her that those two things were the exact same thing. She'd basically just repeated the same thing three times.

"I'm sorry," I apologized, not sounding sincere in the least. "What do you need?"

I might as well listen to her at this point.

She hissed.

"I'm not believin' that you're truly sorry, but whatever." She growled, sounding super pissed.

"I don't really know what you want me to say here," I said. "We're divorced. You continue to call my son, as well as the other members of the MC all the fuckin' time."

"Because you won't answer the phone!" she all but yelled.

"I won't answer the phone because I don't want to talk to you."

Her screech made me pull the phone away from my ear slightly, and that's when Winnie crawled up my body and then planted a wet one directly on my lips.

"What was that?"

I could hear Lizzibeth screaming through the phone an arm's length away.

I sighed and placed the phone back to my ear, despite Winnie being on top of me.

She was running her lips down the length of my jaw, then even farther down my neck to my collarbone.

All the while she let her pussy—her bare pussy—rub against me.

"I'm sorry, what did you ask?"

"You're in bed with her, aren't you?" she hissed.

"I fail to see how that's any of your business," I murmured. "Now, either tell me why you called, or hang up. It's as simple as that."

She made a sound in her throat that even I knew was full of frustration.

Then she started to laugh, making me curious as to what she would say next.

"Well, have fun telling her that you're still married," she hissed. "And good luck getting an easy divorce this time like you did last time. I no longer feel bad for what I did. Not with you cheating on me, also. It ain't gonna happen."

She hung up moments later, and I suddenly realized just why, exactly, Lizzi had been calling as much as she had.

To tell me that we were still married.

I felt like I was going to throw up.

Being married meant a lot of things.

Sort of like she still had access to my property. She still had access to half my money—which wasn't a lot, but it was all I had.

It also meant that the tempting morsel that was on my chest, frozen with her mouth next to my ear—exactly where my phone had previously been resting—would have to wait.

I couldn't have sex with her now that I knew I was still married.

That went against every moral code that I possessed.

Until I found out whether this was true or false, I had to wait...*didn't I?*

Just how, exactly, did that shit happen?

Winnie pulled back and stared into my eyes. The black-out curtains that were covering the windows were doing a piss poor job of what they were designed to do.

"You're still married?"

I let the phone drop from my ear and let it fall to the bed where I tried to breathe deeply to get my anger under control.

"Yeah," I growled. "Or so she says. But lying wasn't really one of Lizzi's problems. She was always upfront with her desires. Such as, she told me point blank that she was going to cheat. I'd thought she was joking. She wasn't."

"Well, shit." She sighed. "Does this mean I can't do you?"

I started to laugh, and it was a surprise. After the news that Lizzibeth had just shared, I didn't think I'd be laughing again...*ever.*

"Yeah, until I figure this out...this means I can't do you."

"Well...shit."

***

At the end of the day, I looked up from loading the boat to see Winnie carefully making her way up the length of the boat, holding on with one hand while she looked down with the other.

These last three days had gone by so well that I questioned why I'd ever told her she couldn't come.

She'd been monumental in making this rescue operation work as well as it had this week.

She'd given a man CPR. She'd helped a woman having a diabetic episode. She'd even held babies while mothers tried to catch a breather.

And I'd fucked her.

I'd. Fucked. Her.

Oh, and I wanted to fuck her again.

A lot.

But until I figured out this shit with Lizzibeth, that wasn't going to happen.

"You okay?"

Winnie looked up and smiled.

"I'm great. I haven't been able to walk for long periods of time without my cane in months. I don't know if it's the water helping me or what, but it's nice to be able to stand without also looking for places to sit in case of an emergency," she answered, making her way to my side.

I looped an arm around her shoulder and pulled her to my side as I continued to tighten the boat's tether to the trailer.

"You want to stop to eat now, or get out of here first?"

She pursed her lips. "I'm thinking we get out of the city first. There's only so many places open, and there's always a line. If we're going to wait anyway, we might as well make headway toward home first."

I agreed, but I wanted to make sure. "Sounds good."

After saying goodbye to the other volunteer police officers, firefighters and medics that had come down and been in our small rescue convoy, we left.

We didn't say a word until we were well outside of the flooded portions of the state.

"You okay?"

Winnie's words had me glancing at her in surprise.

"What?"

"I said are you okay?"

I frowned.

"I'm fine, other than the obvious."

"And what's the obvious?" she pushed.

"The obvious being that Lizzibeth and I had a full annulment," I continued. "We were married for two weeks before she told me that she wasn't a monogamous kind of person."

Winnie blinked. "You're shitting me."

"'Fraid not." I rolled my eyes. "My kid doesn't know this story, so if you happen to speak to him about it, don't share this part." I gave her a wry grin. "She literally told me she was going out on a date while I was on shift, and I didn't believe her. Not until I went into a restaurant to grab a burger during my lunch and found her giggling and laughing, then kissing a man that wasn't me."

"So you divorced her?"

"I thought I did," I confirmed. "I met with a lawyer, we filed it. I signed the papers. She signed the papers. Then the papers were turned in to the county."

"So what happened?" She twirled a stray piece of hair that had fallen from her bun.

"What happened?" I shrugged. "I don't know. I left a message for my lawyer. He's an old friend of mine from the military. Todd said that he would look into it, but hasn't gotten back to me yet."

"It's only been a half a day."

"It has," I agreed.

"I…"

My phone rang, and I hit the answer button on the console. Todd's voice filled the speakers.

"Hey, man," Todd said.

"Todd," I murmured. "I was just talking about you."

"Thought I felt my ears burning." He chuckled. "Hey, did you get my message?"

"Nuh-uh," I said. "Though I've been in a bad area. I'm down south helping out—or was helping out—with the flooding. They had two cell towers go down. What did you have to say?"

"The annulment was denied because apparently the judge had seen you drink before, and he decided that you couldn't be under the influence of alcohol since it could cloud your judgment. And, apparently, with his denial of the annulment, he sent out certified papers to your place and they were signed for by you."

I winced. "I thought they were the annulment papers. Not papers that said that the annulment was denied."

"Anyway," Todd went on. "It was suggested that you file for divorce, which was explained in the papers you received. You had ten days, I believe he said, to file for divorce or the divorce would be dropped off the docket."

"Fuck."

"Yep. So, you want me to file for the divorce?"

I snorted. "Yeah, I do."

"Okay," he said. "I already had all the paperwork drawn up on my part. The only problem is that with divorce, you also have to divide up your assets."

"Our assets," I said carefully.

"Yes," he said. "Anything you bought together while you were married, you have to divide up. Any vehicles, property, or belongings. If she's willing, you can settle this without problem. She signs, you sign. Easy as that. But from what you told me earlier, she probably won't be as willing to do that as she might've once been."

"Yeah," I said. "I've been ignoring her for weeks."

Todd had the decency to quiet his guffaw of laughter by covering the phone, at least.

"Well, stop ignoring her. Try to get her to settle out of court. You know I'll drive over for this if it comes to it, but my wife's been sick the last two weeks, and I'd like to not come down if I don't have to."

"I'll try my best, but it's probably not going to work that way. She was pissed at me."

I looked over at the reason she was pissed at me and winked.

Winnie rolled her eyes.

"Well, I'll file it in the morning. If all goes well, you can have it done within a few weeks."

A few weeks.

I looked back at the woman occupying my passenger seat.

I could make it a few weeks…right?

Yeah, I heard the universe laughing, too.

Lani Lynn Vale

CHAPTER 12

I don't give a sip.
-Coffee Cup

Steel

"But, Mom!"

Winnie's eyes narrowed, and I knew that she was about to blow.

"I told you what I wanted," she snapped. "I realize that you think you're an adult at sixteen years old, but you're not. You're a minor. I am responsible for you until you turn eighteen, or you emancipate yourself from my care. I don't want you to do that, but that threat isn't going to work anymore on me. They're fucking pants. If you don't want to wear them, oh goddamn well. I had to deal with this crap when I was in high school, and never once did I complain. Why? Because I knew the rules. If I didn't like the rules, that was just too goddamn bad. I knew better than to think the rules were going to change just because I didn't like them."

Winnie's daughter's eyes went electric.

"You compare yourself to me all the time. Let me tell you something, *Mom*. Things have changed."

"No, the only thing that has changed is that kids feel entitled to things that they have no right to feel entitled to. What's changed is parents allowing their children to act like assholes by letting them get away with it."

"It's a pair of shorts, Mom."

"NO," she snapped. "It is not. It's a pair of shorts that violates the dress code. The dress code that you violated last week and got sent home for. I don't have time to take off of work to come get you. I especially won't have the desire to come get you when you knew going in that you were violating the dress code. So, here's your choice. You wear jeans, or you wear shorts. Just know that if you're sent home, and I have to come get you, you will be grounded for the next two weeks. In that time, I will throw every single pair of shorts you own in the trash so you have no choice but to wear pants anymore. Also, you can kiss your phone goodbye."

I listened to the two of them argue from my driveway and wondered if I should wade in.

However, with Conleigh not being my daughter—because if she had she would've known better than to try to get away with wearing *those* shorts outside of the house—I had no say so in what was said or done.

Instead, I chilled, waiting for the fight to sputter out.

"Mother, boys sexualize everything. Why should I have to wear pants because they can't control their urges?"

See, here's where I realized that Winnie didn't actually know that I was there, otherwise she wouldn't have said what she said next.

"Are you dense?" Winnie snarled.

"No."

"I think you are."

"I don't think I am."

"Well you are," she said. "Why? Because it has nothing to do with boys not controlling themselves, and everything to do with the fact that it's something that both sexes do equally."

"How do you figure?"

"Because I can't help but look when things are blatant either, and I'm an adult," Winnie snapped. "Just yesterday, Steel walked out of his house without a shirt on, wearing a pair of thin workout shorts. I'm pretty sure he wasn't wearing any underwear because I could see every single piece of his junk. Even though I knew I shouldn't look, I did anyway. Why? Because it was there. I couldn't help it."

Her daughter didn't know what to say.

"So let me ask you this. If Steel had gone into your school wearing that, would you look?"

"First of all," I said from my side of the driveway. "I wouldn't be wearing that to work. And second, I was, in fact, wearing underwear, but thanks for being concerned."

Winnie's mouth dropped open, and her entire face flamed as she looked over at me.

Conleigh started to laugh.

"But she's right," I continued, causing Conleigh's laughter to cut off abruptly. "You wear stuff like that to school, then all the boys are going to look. You're cheapening your worth by wearing it. And, unfortunately, boys will be boys. Just like, if a guy wore what I did the other day—while working out I might add—then the girl would be looking, too."

Conleigh sneered.

"You don't know how it is."

"I know that your mother told you that you couldn't wear that to school," I explained gently. "And I know, had I said the same thing to my mother when I was growing up, my father would've put me down on the ground."

"Well, you're not me," she said. "And parents aren't allowed to hit their children. It's against the law."

Conleigh's eyes moved to me for confirmation.

I suppressed the grin that wanted to break free.

"Actually," I said. "That's up to the parent's discretion. There is a fine line between beating your children just for the hell of it, and using corporal punishment as a form of discipline."

She hissed at me, causing my smile to widen.

"Fine."

Then Conleigh stormed off, leaving us to stare at each other across the street.

"That was fun," I teased.

Winnie flipped me off.

I burst out laughing.

She turned her back on me, then whipped back around and started marching my way.

It'd been exactly a week since we'd been home. A week and a day since I'd had her tight, willing body wrapped around my stiff cock.

She came to a stop directly in front of me, her arms crossed over her chest.

"Are you still married?"

My grin quickly fell.

I knew what she was asking.

Hell, I knew what she was thinking.

I'd been thinking it, too. A lot.

Every single time I saw her get out of her car and walk inside her house…every single time I watched her come outside for something.

It was fucking torture.

I wanted her back in my arms, even though it was the last place in the world she should be.

Little did I know, in twelve short hours, that my entire stance on having her in my arms would change in a single heartbeat.

"Any status updates at least?" Winnie pushed.

I grinned and leaned forward, tucking a stray hair that'd escaped from her slouchy, messy bun on the top of her head behind her ear.

"Lizzibeth is being…difficult," I finally hesitated. "She's decided that she wants half of my estate, one car, and half of my money— including half of my retirement. Oh, and she also wants alimony."

Her mouth dropped open. "You're shitting me."

I shook my head, the rush of anger surging inside of me. "'Fraid not."

Winnie's hands fisted and she stared. "I don't even know what to say to that. Why was it okay before for her to not have any of those things, but now it's suddenly something she wants?"

I shook my head. "We were married for like a week. I brought all of my shit into the relationship. She moved into my house. She had her job, I had mine. We kept our own accounts, always had and would. I had two cars when we married, and she had her one. Hell, I don't even think I've ridden in her car before."

Winnie's face turned calculating.

"Well…" Winnie said. "If she can play that game, so can you."

"What do you mean?"

"She has a house, doesn't she?"

I nodded. "We never sold it. She lives a couple of towns over in a cute little bungalow house with about two acres on it. Horses. Stuff like that."

"Well, I think you should lay claim to those horses, and the house."

I shook my head. "I don't want horses. I wouldn't know what to do with fucking horses."

"Does she know that you don't like horses?"

"Well," I hesitated. "No. The one and only time that she asked me to ride with her, I was called in to work and got out of explaining to her that I was kinda halfway scared to get on one. She hadn't asked again, and I'd taken it as a blessing."

"She likes her horses?" Winnie guessed.

"I can only assume so. She went home every single day to check on them despite having moved in with me and having a neighbor watch after them for her. When I asked her to sell them, she had a mini panic attack."

"She likes them," Winnie confirmed. "Tell her that if she gets half of your stuff, you get half of hers. Make sure to specifically mention horses. Oh, and maybe mention to her that it takes a lot of money to have horses. They require a lot of upkeep. Meaning that she's not hurting for money. What does she do for a living?"

"She's a nurse anesthetist," I answered.

Winnie's eyes went wide. "They make at least one hundred and fifty thousand dollars a year, Steel."

My brows went up. "Yeah?"

Winnie nodded. "Oh yeah, if not more. She has to be smart, too, if she got a job like that. She probably has a pretty good pension going herself. Maybe lay claim to half of that, too. You might also bring up the fact that alimony works both ways. You could actually wind up being the one who gets it since you make less money than her."

I stared at Winnie in surprise. "You're devious. How do you know all of this?"

Winnie's lips thinned. "Just went through it, remember?"

Understanding dawned. "I..."

The front door slammed and Cody ran out, his backpack on his back but the zipper hanging wide open. Each step he took he lost something out of it.

First his folder. Then a library book. A sweatshirt. Papers.

I started to laugh and nodded my head toward him. "Check out your boy."

Winnie turned, saw what was happening, and shook her head.

"Hey, boyo!"

Cody stopped and looked up. "Yeah?"

"You're losing your stuff."

Cody looked behind him where Winnie had gestured, and he threw his hands up in the air. "Awww, man!"

Chuckling under my breath, I waited for Winnie to turn back around before I said, "I'll call her now."

The front door slammed again, and Conleigh's stomping feet could be heard on the porch.

I looked up to see that she was dressed in jeans and a t-shirt that said "Buck" on it. I shook my head and returned my eyes to her mother.

Winnie sighed and fished her keys out of her front pocket. "You do that. I gotta get these kids to school."

"Have fun at work."

She held her thumb up. "Will do. You, too."

My lips twitched as I watched her walk away. Then I pulled my phone out and placed a call to Lizzibeth.

"I'm not budging on the alimony or the car," she greeted me.

I watched Winnie start her car and then Cody and Conleigh pile in before she backed out and accelerated down the street.

Then I went about explaining what was going to happen now.

"Is that what you want me to do?"

"Those horses are mine. They were mine before we married, and you don't like horses. You even said so multiple times when we were married."

"I don't remember saying that," I agreed. "But I'm finding a sudden fondness for them now."

"Fuck you," Lizzibeth snarled.

"Sign the fucking papers."

Then I hung up and got into my cruiser and drove to work with a huge fucking smile on my face.

CHAPTER 13

Being an ugly woman is like being a man. You're going to have to work.
-Things not to say to a woman

Winnie

The creeper was in the ER, and it only took one second after he gave me his name for me to understand exactly why the man had given me the creeps in the first place.

"Anderson Munnick."

I shuddered as I processed his name.

"And can you tell me why you're here …" I trailed off as the name finally sank home.

Anderson Munnick. The man that had followed me home. The same man that I'd testified against.

The same man that had been in prison for ten years.

The same man that I was supposed to be notified about if and when he ever got out of prison.

Ten fucking years.

He only had to serve ten fucking years? What the absolute *fuck*?

And then the fear started to sink into my bones.

I couldn't defend myself. Conleigh was a young girl of age. She was fucking beautiful. She looked exactly like me but still in her prime. The exact same type of girl Anderson Munnick liked.

My stomach convulsed.

I stood up so fast that my chair kept going and hit the wall behind me.

"Get out," I hissed.

"I'm not getting out," he disagreed, leaning back calmly in his seat. "My, my, have you changed. You put on weight. Tisk-tisk."

I had put on all of three pounds since he saw me, three of those pounds being in the last year due to my lack of exercise.

But he wasn't really caring that I put on weight. He only wanted me to know that he noticed that I did. That he paid close attention to my body.

"Get. Out," I repeated.

"But I have a cut on my hand." He held up his hand to show me.

The cut on his hand was tiny. Miniscule. A single tiny slash that was already starting to clot.

A papercut at most.

"Get out," I repeated.

"Think the lady said to get the hell out."

I had never, not in my life, felt so relieved to see a man who had denied me a job.

But there Sean was, and I instantly sagged in relief.

Sean was former military, jacked, and intimidating…also, highly protective for some reason.

His eyes took in everything in a glance, and before I could so much as explain what was going on, he was standing between me and Anderson.

"Go," Sean repeated.

"This is a county hospital," Anderson smiled. "Funded by the county. That means that I have a right to be seen here."

"She also has a right to screen you out," Sean said. "Because it's a waste of county tax money. Trust me on this, go before the police get here."

Anderson's eyes narrowed.

"I know my rights," he said. "And I'm having chest pains now."

He clutched at his chest and feigned—poorly, might I add—pain.

That was when the doctor came in, looking highly upset.

"Winnie, what's going on here?" Dr. Stratton asked carefully.

"This man came in for a papercut on his finger. I informed him that he would likely be screened out, and now he's feigning chest pain."

Dr. Stratton was not my favorite doctor. In fact, if I could name one doctor that I would never, ever want to work on me, it'd be him.

If I came into the ER—emergency room—with a broken arm and he walked in, I'd get my shit and leave. He had a terrible bedside manner, was condescending to anyone he felt was 'lower' than him, like me, and made disgusting jokes when it was least appropriate.

"Well, if he's having chest pains, you know we can't turn him away. Bring him back, start an IV, and then get a couple of leads on him so we can run an EKG," Dr. Stratton instructed.

I shook my head. "I can't treat him."

"Then why are you here?" Dr. Stratton snarled.

I opened my mouth to reply when the charge nurse on call made her way into the tiny room as well.

Overall the room was eight feet by eight feet with a desk in the middle of the room. Behind the desk stood me, Dr. Stratton, and Tally Tomirkanivov—the charge nurse. Sean was in front of me, and then Anderson on the other side of the desk.

Outside of the tiny cubicle room stood two of the security guards that were stationed across from my room in case a patient got unruly.

All the while, Anderson smirked.

"He's faking it," Sean boomed, startling me. "I watched him antagonize Winnie, and when she asked him to leave, he faked his new condition. Trust me on this, he ain't hurtin'."

"Unfortunately, you can't be sued if you're wrong. The hospital, however, can be. We have no choice but to take him in and check him over. Now, Winnie, do your job."

I ground my teeth together and almost refused.

Almost.

But then I saw the smug look on Anderson's face.

He would be happy if I refused and then got fired.

I saw it in his eyes.

So I steeled my spine and gestured to the door. "After you."

***

Steel

I brought a suspect in to get checked over, and walked in to see Sean, Tally—Tommy Tom's wife, Tommy Tom—also a member of the MC, Naomi—Sean's wife, and Ellen—Jessie James' wife who also happened to be a member of the MC, all standing in the entrance of the ER.

They were whispering furiously about something, but Sean kept looking toward the back of the room as if something back there was of supreme interest to him.

"What's going on?" I asked, shoving my perp at an ER tech. "Can you take him and get him cleaned up?"

He nodded and gestured to the first open bed which was about eight feet from me.

My eyes turned back to the group, and I could see that Sean was extremely pissed.

"What's up?" I asked, then frowned. "Since when do you two work together again?"

Sean and Naomi were both paramedics; however, since they'd gotten married they weren't allowed to be partners any longer. Now they both worked opposite shifts except for one time a week—which wasn't today because otherwise, I'd be watching their children.

"I was called in to work," Naomi explained. "And since the kids are at daycare, I went ahead and did it. I should be done by five, though, in time to pick them up."

I nodded. "Okay, now tell me what's going on."

That's when I saw Winnie in the room across the expanse of the large, open ER...with the same man that I'd forced onto the bus during the hurricane only a few days ago.

"What the fuck?"

I didn't wait for them to explain, only charged across the room and came to a bone-jarring halt next to Winnie's side.

She jumped a foot in the air when I appeared beside her, and the little fucker on the bed started to guffaw.

"What the fuck?" I said. "Why are you here?"

"I'm hurt, Officer. Really hurt. I'm having chest pains."

He didn't look like he was having chest pains. He looked like he was sitting pretty in the ER for reasons unknown. The little fucker wasn't hurt in any way. Hurt people didn't smile when they were getting an IV placed in their arm.

Winnie finished placing the IV and then threw all her trash away before washing her hands.

"Your doctor will be in with you in a minute," Winnie said, then took hold of my hand.

I gave the stupid 'patient' one more angry look, which he volleyed back with a laughing one of his own and a thumb up, before following her out the door.

Once she was out of the cubicle, she pulled the curtains, then trudged forward.

She not only passed the ER, but then she went even farther past the group still gathered at the door and continued until she was outside the ER entrance altogether.

"It's him."

I blinked. "Him who?"

"Him." She repeated. "The man I sent to jail. I finally realized why he was so familiar to me. He's the man I testified against."

"Are you sure?" I questioned. "It's customary for someone to call regarding the release of a person that someone testified against. You didn't get any calls letting you know that he was out?"

She shook her head. "Could he have called Matt? I haven't received anything in regards to him getting out. Not a phone call.

Not a letter. Nothing. The detective promised me that if he ever got out, he'd let me know. He was sincere, but this," she gestured to the ER with her hand. "Caught me off guard. And he's enjoying the fact."

I gritted my teeth and tried to gain my composure.

"Only one way to find out," I growled, then placed the phone to my ear.

Two minutes later, I was listening to Matt try to explain away why he hadn't informed Winnie of the man she'd testified against getting out of jail.

"I meant to," Matt explained. "But we were on bad terms."

"You were on bad terms," I repeated. "If the situation were reversed, and this had happened to you, would you care if there were bad terms between you and Winnie if she had important information pertaining to your safety to tell you? You let her down, allowed her to get caught off guard. Had we known that he was getting out, we could've filed a restraining order against him preemptively. But you didn't let her know, and she was not only blindsided today at the hospital, but she was also ambushed in the dark while we were down south helping with hurricane relief. She could've been killed because of you."

"Don't put this on me," Matt countered.

"This *is* on you. You've known he was getting out for a month. The detective in charge of this case sent you a certified letter *and* called you. He trusted you, as Winnie's former husband, to relay the news. Something he wouldn't have done if you hadn't said that you would. She could've been raped or killed, Matt."

Winnie lost all color in her face, and I cursed again as I reached forward and hooked one arm around her back, pulling her to me.

If she fell, I'd at least catch her.

My eyes scanned the area as I spoke with the dipshit on the phone, listening to his pathetic excuses for allowing his ex-wife to be in danger, and found my eyes focusing on the glass windows that blanketed the automatic doors.

And found not just my son watching me, but Tommy Tom, Tally, Ellen, and Naomi as well.

I rolled my eyes as they watched us, whispering like the little children that they were.

Gossips. *All of them.*

"Bring me the information to my office by end of the day, and Matt?"

"Yeah?" Matt asked warily.

"You have a duty to Winnie. You may not be married to her any longer, but as a decent human being and an officer of the law, you should've let her in on this. At the very least, if you were on such bad terms with her, you should have told me or another officer to tell her. If anything happens to her, Matt, that's on you."

Winnie shivered in my arms, and I squeezed her tight before hanging up the phone.

"I can't say that I'm surprised by the fact that he kept this from me," Winnie admitted.

"Me either," I grumbled. "Me either."

The sliding glass doors opening had us all turning to look.

It'd been a little over twenty minutes since we'd exited the hospital, and apparently, that was enough time for Anderson Munnick to realize that he wasn't getting the attention that he required.

"Sir!" A nurse followed him out. "You can't leave. If you leave, you'll be AMA—against medical advice—and won't be readmitted."

Anderson scoffed. "Like I care."

"You'll be flagged," Winnie said. "When you leave AMA, they don't like that. You'll be labeled as a dumbass and they won't allow you in unless you're obviously having an actual emergency that's visible. You won't get to just walk in like you did today and get seen."

Anderson saw Winnie in my arms, and his eyes went wide, while his smile dimmed.

"Is that right?" he asked, coming to a stop about four feet from us, crossing his arms over his chest.

The bad thing was, Anderson Munnick was quite appealing. I could see how women would be attracted to him. Why did he have to rape to get a woman?

And we all knew that he was a rapist.

I'd looked him up once I got back home a few days ago in the police database.

He was charged with only one count of rape but was also suspected of not just a few, but many more. They couldn't actually pin anything else on him due to lack of evidence in the other cases, and it was only Winnie's testimony that had tied him to the location of the rape that he was convicted of. Who knew what he'd been doing since he was out.

The automatic doors opened, but I didn't take my gaze off of Anderson long enough to see who'd come out.

But when I felt the familiar hand of my son on my shoulder, I felt an inner peace that allowed me to calm down.

"Time to leave, buddy."

"You can't tell me to leave. I'm standing in a parking lot."

"Loitering," I murmured, gesturing to a state police car that was pulling into the lot. "Which I'm sure we can find a way to take you in for. It'll be fun…how about you continue. Any arrest, even loitering, is a violation of your parole. Which then means you'll be heading back."

"They won't send me back to jail because I was loitering," Anderson countered.

Aaron pulled up in his cruiser and got out, leaving the door open as he did.

He didn't say a word, but he didn't need to. His presence was enough to cause that extra little bit of worry that I needed for Anderson to leave.

Sometimes I hated being a cop.

I hated standing here with my hands tied behind my back. I hated the fact that I couldn't just walk up to the motherfucker and punch him in the face, threaten his ass to stay away from my woman.

Everything came screeching to a halt inside my mind. *My woman?*

"Do you want to find out?" Sean asked, stealing the words from my mouth. "Because that's what is about to happen. Personally, I think you should give it a try. See how it goes."

There were times when my son was younger that I didn't appreciate his smart-ass mouth, but now that he was older, I could find the humor in it.

Like now.

"Time to go," I said. "Either leave or get arrested."

Anderson sneered at me, my son, and then stopped when his eyes landed on Winnie.

Or more particularly, Winnie's head.

She wasn't looking at Anderson. She was looking at the crowd that I could feel gathered behind my back.

My family.

"See you soon, sweet Winnie."

Winnie ignored him, but I didn't.

I charged forward, pushing Winnie from my arms, and stopped inches from the little fucker's face.

"Listen here, Anderson," I said quietly. "Don't give me a reason to do this. Don't. Because you will not win. You might think you will, but you won't. I'm older, wiser and have a lot more experience in this life shit than you do. Don't be stupid. Get out of town, stop raping women and live your life. Trust me on this."

Anderson's eyes narrowed. "I don't rape women, Chief. They ask for what I do to them."

I wanted to plant my fist in the little asshole's face.

I contained myself. Barely.

"Think on what I said. But get out of here while you do it."

CHAPTER 14

Forgive your enemy, but remember the bastard's name.
-Something you probably shouldn't say to a five-year-old

Winnie

My eyes took in the two stray dogs that were running on the side of the road, and I kept them there as I tried not to yell at my kid once again.

However, when we pulled into the Dixie Wardens' clubhouse moments later, my cool had again evaporated.

Conleigh trudged behind us, pissed off that I was forcing her to miss a day with her friends to instead spend it with me, her brother and Steel.

She didn't give one single shit that we were meeting Steel's friends.

All she cared about was that she had some money, thanks to a job that Steel had gotten her at the police department of all places, and wasn't going to get to spend the cash she'd made over the last week.

Not to mention that because of her anger toward me, I'd taken her phone away. The phone that she'd been using to talk to a boy on for the first four hours of the day. Which had then set her off all over again.

"How long do we have to stay?" Conleigh hissed at my back.

Steel looked down at me, caught my anger, and winked.

I rolled my eyes and turned my head so I could look over my shoulder. "As long as I feel like staying, Conleigh, and not a moment before."

She growled at me under her breath, and her brother jumped in.

"You sound like a bear," Cody observed.

"She's acting like one, too."

"Thanks, Mom," Conleigh snarled.

My lips twitched when Steel gave me a laughing look.

I guess that was what it would take not to take Conleigh's attitude personally.

When Steel was around, she was an angel. Literally, there was the child that Conleigh was when Steel was around, and the one that she was when we were alone.

Sure, she'd complained in front of him when we'd had the verbal smackdown after she'd tried to wear daisy dukes to school, but eventually Conleigh had gotten her act together and had changed. Today? Well, today she was still the girl that I knew and loved…even though sometimes her attitude made me question my sanity.

Conleigh had shared her anger far and wide, and even Steel, her very best advocate, didn't get spared.

She'd raged at him right along with me, accusing him of being the antichrist, and then informed him that 'his shit stank just like the rest of the population.'

She was still bitching, moaning and complaining as we walked through the front doors.

And then she came to a halt right inside the doors, just as I did.

Her reasoning was likely due to the hunky looking man boy standing in our way. Mine was due to the fact that Steel's face had split into a wide smile as he threw his arms around the boy and said, with great affection, "Linc!"

I found myself grinning, even though I had no clue who this *Linc* character was.

What I did know was that he was tall, toned, and in fucking awesome shape. He had a beard, his hair was on the longer side, and he was a near body double for Jessie James—one of the members of the MC that Steel belonged to.

My lips twitched when I got a look at my daughter's face.

I looked over to Steel to gauge his reaction, and I saw the moment he realized that Conleigh was enamored. The man missed nothing.

"Linc," Steel said, stepping away from him and shifting sideways to allow Linc to see us more fully. "This is my woman, Winnie, her daughter, Conleigh, and Cody, her son."

It took a few moments for me to process what, exactly, was said, but when I did, my eyes widened right along with my daughter's.

Linc caught both and started to chuckle. "Y'all could pass as sisters."

We got that a lot. I would've told him so, too, but I was still stuck on Steel's declaration.

My woman.

My. Woman.

Winnie, Steel's woman. That was me—*he was referring to me!*

Steel caught my reaction and started to grin, but before he could say anything else, kids came out of the woodwork and started to pat Steel's pant legs.

I backed away as more and more came and then started to laugh when he bent down to their level.

They loved him. Every last one of them.

"So…Steel and you?"

I looked over at my daughter, who'd whispered to me, "Uhhh, yeah. I…yeah…"

Conleigh smiled at me for the first time that day.

"I like it, Mom. I'm glad. Steel is a good guy and doesn't freak out when I do something stupid." She paused. "But, Mom?"

"Yeah?"

"I thought I heard you say the other day on the phone with Krisney that Steel was still married."

I winced. "It was a mix-up," I began to explain, not leaving anything out.

I didn't want Conleigh to think that I would ever condone this had the situation not been as it was. I wasn't a cheater, and it didn't matter if you were as hot as Steel was. I had standards, unlike my ex-husband.

"Steel isn't a cheater."

I looked up to find Linc, who was incredibly good at blending into the woodwork, staring at us. He'd obviously heard every word that we'd discussed.

"I know," I agreed softly.

His eyes turned to Conleigh. "You can trust him. He once came and got me when I was drunk off my ass and hours away from my college acceptance conference. He sobered me up, got me cleaned up and dressed, and then dropped me off in time for the televised event. All of that without telling my dad. He's trustworthy, and you won't find a better man to have your back."

Conleigh took every single word in that he said to her and then smiled.

Linc's body went taut and that was when I realized that Conleigh's appreciation of him was not only reciprocated but possibly even more disadvantageous on his end.

Shit.

Conleigh, my beautiful girl, was only sixteen.

However, she'd had to grow up fast. Since she was a young girl, she'd had to do things that a normal child wouldn't have to do. Such as stay on her own when she was really much too young to be allowed on her own while I worked. She'd been cooking for herself since she was tall enough to work a microwave, and not a day went by that she didn't try to pay for something that a child shouldn't be paying for.

She had a good head on her shoulders, so I wasn't worried in the least that they'd do something stupid.

But, as I watched Linc gesture for us to follow him away from the crowd of kids who still hadn't let up, I realized that neither one of them were stupid.

That didn't mean that the attraction that I could practically feel moving between them might not outweigh their common sense.

I'd have to talk to Steel, as well as Conleigh.

From what Steel had told me, Linc was a freshman at LSU and on the fast track to the NFL once he was eligible for the draft, which made him eighteen or nineteen. That was a two-to-three-year age difference between the two of them.

But, at least I'd started talking to Conleigh early about things like STDs, birth control, pregnancy, and money problems. I didn't spare her the gritty details at all.

I was very blunt and upfront with my girl.

"Mommy?"

As they walked away, my son stopped me with a tug on my arm as I wondered if she'd use the common sense that God gave her and would hopefully not act like I did when I was her age.

"Yeah, baby?" I asked.

"Is that a wolf?"

I looked over at a dog that did, indeed, look like a wolf.

"Uhhh," I hesitated.

"Part wolf."

I looked over to see the older version of the boy who'd just walked off with my daughter and grinned.

"It's cute," I said. "But I thought they were illegal."

Jessie shrugged, his eyes going to where his son was now standing on the back deck reaching into a cooler. He came back up with a Dr. Pepper and handed it to Conleigh. "Sooo…"

I burst out laughing. "Yeah, so…"

He snorted, then held his hand out to me.

I took it as he introduced himself.

"I know who you are," I said. "I was in the police cruiser with Steel a few days ago when you pulled up next to us at a stop light. It's nice to officially meet you."

I'd also seen him from afar at the hospital when, on the rare occasion, he came to visit his wife, Ellen.

Speaking of Ellen, she came sauntering up, a half glass of wine clutched in her hand and a mutilated sandwich in the other.

"Uhh," I said. "Were you hungry?"

Ellen snorted. "My daughter has decided that anything other than the crust is the devil on sandwiches. Last week, she'd only eat the filling, sans bread. I guess we're making progress."

I grinned.

"Cody," I placed my hand on Cody's head, who was very interested in the wolf-dog at the moment. "Went through this phase where he'd eat only meat. I couldn't get him to touch a vegetable or a carb to save my life for about six months."

Ellen chuckled as she handed Cody the sandwich. "Tell him to sit, and then give it to him."

Cody took the sandwich without flinching, his interest in the pup too great.

He loved dogs. The two that we'd seen on our way to the clubhouse had been fussed over, quite a bit, as we'd driven.

"Sit," Cody ordered the pup.

The 'dog' sat, and Cody handed him the food between his fingers.

My belly clenched when I saw the dog lean forward quickly, horror filling my veins, but all the dog did was gently take the food, and then swallow it whole.

"Shit," I muttered. "That just scared the crap out of me."

"Oh, don't worry about my baby. He would never hurt anybody who wasn't deserving of it. I can't say that about any other dog, though."

I agreed.

Working in the ER was enlightening, to say the least.

There was at least one dog bite a week, and sometimes they were *really* bad. It'd left a bad taste in my mouth, so I was wary of nearly every dog, small or big, now.

"Did you hear about the one last week?"

I nodded.

While I'd been gone, a young girl that was all of eighteen months old had been mauled by the family poodle. The poodle had mauled her before the parents could so much as react. She'd been flown to a neighboring hospital where she'd immediately undergone emergency surgery, but her face would never be the same.

"I did." I frowned. "What were those parents doing while their dog was biting their kid's face?"

"I don't even know." She shook her head. "It was awful."

I could imagine.

"What's awful?"

Steel threaded his arm around my back and pulled me into his chest, and I couldn't help the sappy smile that lit my face.

Steel was hot and hard all over, and I wanted to bury my face in his neck and inhale his scent.

I managed to contain myself because of my son only a few feet away from me.

"A dog bite."

Steel grunted. "I had to deal with that one when I got back. The parents will likely be charged. Kid's fucked up for life."

I rolled my eyes at Steel's eloquent use of words.

"Yeah, I'm sure." I frowned. "Did you go see the child?"

He nodded once. "Yeah. She's got a long road ahead of her, that's for sure."

Terrible.

"Mommy, I want a dog."

I snorted. "I can't get a dog right now, buddy. Maybe next year."

Cody gave me a look that clearly said what he thought about my lie.

"You said that last year."

Steel started to chuckle.

I shot him a mock glare, and he winked, causing my heart to flip over in my chest.

"Are y'all going to have a baby?"

Startled, I looked over at my son and immediately started to shake my head.

"Ummm, no," I disagreed. "You and Conleigh are all I need, and Steel has a son that could very well be your father. Trust me, kids aren't ever in the cards for us."

Steel squeezed my hip. "Plus," he drawled. "You're a handful. I'm not sure we could handle having another kid like you." Then he looked at me with alarm. "Maybe I should get fixed."

Wasn't that the truth.

"What does fixed mean?" Cody questioned.

I held my smile in check. "It means that he would no longer have the necessary products to achieve making a baby anymore."

Jessie started to laugh as he tugged his wife's hand. "Let's go. Watching them try to explain this to a young kid is like watching a train wreck."

"Just wait," Steel called after their retreating forms. "You'll have to have this talk with your own kids soon!"

That I didn't argue with. They would. Every parent eventually had to.

It was always painful and likely always would be.

"Can we go get ice cream after we leave here?"

My eye twitched.

"The speed in which you change subjects makes my head spin," Steel murmured. "Are you hungry? There are hot dogs."

"Steel?"

Cody's quiet words had Steel dropping down beside my son, his face serious. "Yeah, buddy?"

"Did you know that the average human body holds enough bones to make a human skeleton?"

At that, Steel wasn't the only one to burst out laughing. We all did.

All of us but Cody.

That was my boy, though. He loved spouting off useless facts, even if sometimes he didn't understand them.

"Yeah," Steel said once he had himself under control. "I think I did know that."

Cody patted Steel's cheek. "I don't like hot dogs. Is there any steak?"

Steel took Cody's hand and walked off, leaving me to watch after them with a smile on my face.

"Careful."

I looked up to find Fender standing next to me now.

"About what?"

"I see you falling."

I blinked.

"I don't know what you're talking about," I hedged.

There was no falling. I'd already fallen. I was literally head over heels in love with the man, and there wasn't a single thing I could do about it.

Lani Lynn Vale

CHAPTER 15

And you thought my beard was big.
-T-shirt

Steel

"Where's Winnie?" I asked Tally.

Tally pointed in the direction of the breakroom.

"Eating lunch," she said, eyes on a chart. "Don't keep her too long. She has to be back for Peter to take his lunch, and he likes to whine to the charge nurse—me—if he doesn't get his full hour."

I snorted. "I'll see what I can do."

Tally looked up over the rim of some reading glasses and glared. "I'm serious, Big Papa. I have like, eight hundred thousand things to do, and listening to him whine is not one of them. He's seriously the worst."

My brows rose at that. "Okay."

She narrowed her eyes. "Why don't I believe you?"

I shrugged. "I've never steered you wrong before, have I, Tally?"

Tally snorted, and I chose to take that answer as a no, before I walked down the hall to the break room.

My eyes scanned the area as I walked, and I nodded my head at Tommy Tom, who saw me through the part in one of the curtained off rooms.

I stopped and turned, then went back to the room where Tommy Tom was holding up an X-ray film in the air below a light.

"Tommy Tom?"

He looked over at me while still holding the film in the air.

"Yeah?"

"You got keys to the break room?" I questioned.

He shook his head.

"What about a supply closet?"

He pulled out a set of keys and tossed them to me.

"No, but I do have keys to my office. You know where it is," he answered.

I grinned as I caught the keys.

"Thanks," I muttered, turning on my booted feet and marching toward the break room at a much faster pace.

Contrary to what Tally thought, I wouldn't make Winnie late. However, I never said anything about not getting her messy.

I just hoped that she'd finished her meal because I had plans for the rest of her lunchtime.

Which—I lifted my wrist—by my count, was about twenty-two minutes.

I'd tried to get here earlier so I could share that lunch with her, but I'd been held up writing not one, not two, but three tickets on my way to the hospital. One was to a teenager who was barely out of diapers, another was a single mother—who I let off with a written warning solely because she had a screaming infant in the back seat—and then there was the dick with the black, jacked up truck. Chicks could be dicks, right?

This woman in her big black truck had refused to allow me to cross the street with Cody this morning, and then, this afternoon, when I'd seen her blow past a stop sign, I'd taken it as a perfectly good sign from above that she needed a ticket.

When I ran her plates, I saw that her tags were expired. So not only did she get a ticket for running a stop sign, she also got one for her expired tags—*and* expired insurance.

Though, she assured me that she actually did have updated insurance cards, just not with her.

I wrote the ticket anyway, and then she flipped me off and called me a pig.

That was just the icing on the cake of my already shitastic day.

I needed Winnie in my arms. I wanted to hold her. I wanted to bury my face in her hair and inhale. I just plain wanted her…which downright scared me.

I never needed a woman.

Women were pains in the asses—my ass especially.

I didn't have the time, nor the inclination to deal with them, yet I was finding myself making an exception for Winnie.

I wanted her in my life. Hell, I even wanted her children in my life.

Which was why I'd taken Cody to school that day despite her assuring me I didn't have to.

It was also why I'd thrown Conleigh's name at the head of circulation and asked her to find room in her department for Conleigh to work part-time.

I pushed through the door to the break room and immediately my gaze honed in on Winnie.

She was leaning her backside against the counter, her face lost in thought.

The moment the sound of the door registered to her, she looked up, and her face broke out into a smile before she was running toward me.

"I thought you weren't going to make it?" she questioned, rubbing her face on my uniform shirt.

I rumbled something deep in my throat and wrapped my arms around Winnie's upper body and head, pulling her in a little tighter as I said, "Didn't think I was going to, either. However, your favorite ex-husband took over my area for me so I could grab a quick bite to eat."

Winnie leaned her head back and stared at me with a small smile on her face. "Favorite ex-husband. He could also be labeled as 'biggest asshole ex-husband,'" she pointed out.

I laughed as I dropped my lips to hers, and she gladly took the kiss.

I felt her hand tighten on the loop of my belt at the small of my back, and I drew in a breath.

"You think you can run with me to Tommy's office? I have something I want to show you," I murmured against her lips.

She pulled back and away as she nodded once.

My eyes trailed down her scrub top, and I barely contained the grin that threatened to turn my lips up.

"Cold?"

She punched me in the chest, and I grunted.

"Ow!" I said, rubbing at the hurt with two knuckles.

"You wouldn't have even felt that if you were wearing your Kevlar vest," she pointed out.

That I knew.

Although, there was nothing I could do about it. Not without having the money for me to do it.

One day I'd get one, but for now, I'd continue to live like I was living.

I tugged on Winnie's hand and said, "I spoke with the treasurer about it like you asked. They're going to try to locate the funds."

Winnie stayed at my side while I unlocked the door to Tommy's office and then looked around curiously as I pushed it open and flipped the light on.

"What are you…"

The door to the office was kicked shut, relocked, and then up against Winnie's back in a matter of moments.

"Steel," she gasped. "What are you…"

I took her mouth then, tangling my tongue with hers, forcing her jaw up to take more of me.

"Steel," she gasped. "What are you…"

She tried to repeat the same words when I let her up for air, but I just shook my head.

"But…"

I shoved my hand up the outside of her shirt and fisted her bra strap with my hand.

"Tommy Tom won't come in," I told her, moving my lips down the length of her neck. "And if you don't focus, we're going to have to stop what we're doing."

"What are we doing?"

"We're about two pants and a set of panties away from fucking."

"You're not wearing underwear?"

I grinned. "I had to change my pants at work because a suspect thought it'd be funny to take a piss on himself—which then ended up on me when I had to tackle him to the ground."

Her face went pinched. "Gross."

"Gross," I agreed, then started to work her shirt up over her head.

She willingly allowed me to remove it, then went ahead and did the hard work by shucking her shoes, and then her pants as well as panties.

The only thing she had left on was her bra and her socks.

She looked fucking adorable.

"Pick me up," she ordered.

That adorableness turned to sexiness in a blink of an eye.

"Yes, ma'am," I teased, leaning down.

She threaded her arms around my neck and I lifted her up so that her face was level with mine.

"Don't put that pussy on my pants," I ordered. "I can't walk around with a stained crotch. I have nothing else to change into."

She bit her lip as her eyes sparkled. "Then I suggest that you lose the pants."

I winked and reached between us, slowly unhooking my utility belt and lowering it to the floor before starting in on my pants.

Moments later they were down around my ankles and she was grinding herself down against me.

"Not that I don't like this," she said, pressing her lips against my throat, right above where my pulse sped. "But what caused this to come on? You're usually a stickler for the rules."

She was right. I was usually fairly adamant about keeping things professional and putting on a good face for my city.

However, today had been bad.

Not only had I had to deal with Mr. Pissy Pants and big black truck girl, but I'd also had to listen to the judge tell me that he thought Lizzibeth and I should go to mediation.

When I'd flat out refused that, he said arbitration might be the only viable alternative.

Which led to me calling Lizzibeth and giving her twenty-four hours to sign the divorce papers, or I would stop playing nice.

My guess was that she'd call my bluff, but I wasn't bluffing.

I was pissed off, fed up, and I wanted to fuck my woman without a goddamn guilty conscience.

I knew that Winnie didn't care. She understood. However, I felt wrong fucking her when my almost ex-wife was still in the picture—even if it was from a distance.

"Lizzibeth," I answered, feeling her stiffen.

"Bitch."

Then she reached between us, wrapped her small hand around my cock, and then guided it to her entrance.

I didn't know what the hell I was thinking when I thought I could deny the sexual attraction between the two of us. I must've been out of my goddamned mind, that was for sure.

Because the moment she sank onto me, her entire pussy engulfing my cock, I realized how futile my resistance was.

She was what my body craved, and who the hell was I to deny her anything?

"Steel…"

"Had a bad day." I pronounced that statement by thrusting my cock into her.

Feeling her tighten around me, there was a wave of instant rightness of the act. I knew that this was where I was supposed to be and it made my shitty morning disappear.

Here, inside Winnie, nothing else mattered. Not my very soon-to-be ex-wife. Not work. Not anything. Only her. Only us.

I came here straight from pulling over that bitch in her big truck. The only thing on my mind was erasing my morning.

Winnie was the perfect fucking eraser. My eraser.

She was the only person in my life who brought me peace. My son, my grandchildren, the members of my club—they're my family, my everything. But they all made demands of me and my time.

Winnie, though?

She didn't demand anything of me. She listened to me, and she paid attention. She soothed and calmed me. She comforted and cherished me. No one else in my life, past or present, gave me all of that.

Winnie was it—she was the woman I'd been searching for.

"Steel, please."

I looked into her eyes as I used the strength in my shoulders and arms to slowly slide her up.

I held her there momentarily while she whimpered for my cock, and then I lowered her onto me.

Her mouth curved into an O as I thrust up on the downward glide, filling her with me again.

My cock became more and more sensitive with each drive into her until it throbbed. Slide up. Throb. Glide down. Throb. Slide up, throb, glide down.

Our eyes stayed connected., never once losing sight of each other. At least until I felt her muscles start to tighten around me.

Her pupils dilated, and she lost focus of what was in front of her—me.

This glazed look overtook her, and I watched as she fell apart.

The need I had for her was all consuming, and the fact that she got there with just a few words, a kiss and my cock, ramped up everything I was feeling.

Also knowing that she was there, I loosened the strings on my control.

The come in my balls felt like it boiling. The tight, wet fist of her pussy erased everything but the thought of me coming from my mind.

And then I was. I detonated and emptied myself inside her in three long bursts.

Moments later, we were both breathing hard. I was sweating up a storm, and Winnie was looking at me with amusement in her eyes.

"Not that I mind erasing your bad morning…but what happened to make it bad?" she whispered, smoothing her hand down my bearded cheek.

I grunted something under my breath and patted her legs that were still wrapped around me.

She took the hint and dropped them to the floor.

Pulling out of her, I immediately grinned and winked.

"I'll get something to clean you up," I said as I bent down and reached for my pants.

She waited patiently as I tucked myself back inside of my pants and zipped them up.

I snatched a couple tissues off the corner of Tommy Tom's desk and handed them to her.

She took them and cleaned herself up while I glanced around the office.

I'd never been in here before, which then cracked me up seeing as the first time I was, it was to use it for sex. It didn't have anything at all to do with the man who the office belonged to.

"What are you laughing at?" Winnie asked, bending over to grab her scrub pants off the floor.

I explained moments later, causing her to grin.

"Yeah," she snickered. "I've never been in here before, either. I actually wondered where he disappeared to sometimes when his wife was around and not working."

I just shook my head and chuckled as I walked toward her.

She finished slipping her feet into her shoes without tying them and then lifted her face up toward me with a smile.

I dropped one final kiss on her cheek before I said, "Grab those tissues and trash them in the bathroom when you go…I have to go back to work."

She sighed and then pulled away as far as the door at her back would let her.

"Try to have a better day?"

I shrugged. "Seems like this full moon is fucking with everyone and everything. Not to mention Aaron had the nerve to mention something about it being fucking 'quiet' today."

Winnie started to laugh and reached for the door, twisting the knob and opening it.

I stepped back and allowed her to do so before following her out of it moments later.

She'd just made it to the bathroom, with five minutes to spare, when I stopped her.

"Winnie?"

"Yeah?" She turned, her eyes sparkling.

I opened my mouth to tell her what I was feeling but was interrupted by the mic at my shoulder going off. "Shooting at South and High."

I sighed and pinched my nose.

"If I make it back in time, I'll come over for dinner."

"Is that your way of telling me that you'd like me to cook?" she teased.

But the smile that she'd forced onto her face didn't meet her eyes. She was worried.

Which then caused a small amount of exhilaration to surge through my veins.

"Yeah, baby," I said, crowding her into the door and laying one more kiss on her lips. "It is."

Then I left and didn't look back.

CHAPTER 16

I'd take a Nerf bullet for you.
-Winnie to Steel

Steel

"There are rules," I said to the kid beside me. He may not be old enough to understand all of what I was saying to him just yet, but he was old enough to listen. Especially with the way he sucked in knowledge like a sponge. For instance, the useless facts that he picked up and then regurgitated whenever he felt like it.

Most of the time, the useless facts he'd spout weren't relevant to the situation, but for Cody, we didn't mind. He was the cutest kid on the planet, even my own son hadn't been that cute.

So, I spoke, telling him the way of a man in this world, just like I'd done, a long time ago, with my own son. "One, you never shake a man's hand while sitting down."

"Shake?"

I reached out and took his hand in mine, my big hand engulfing his much smaller one. "Shake. Like this."

"Shake!" He nodded. "I know how to do that."

I grinned and let his hand go, not caring in the least that my hand was now sticky like his had been.

He asked for a popsicle when we walked in the house together a few minutes earlier, and I'd thought nothing of it.

What I hadn't expected was for the boy to be so messy. Seriously, at the age of five, I don't remember Sean being as dirty as this one...but then again, I never really let Sean have popsicles, either.

"Another rule is that you always eat lunch with the new kid. You will never know if that new kid is your best friend if you don't put yourself out there."

"Yes. I sat with Etan last week. He moved from Canananada." He agreed. "What else?"

Etan was actually Ethan. He wasn't from Canada, though. He was from the Great Lakes area but had traveled with his father on business trips often that took him across the border.

Cody headed toward me and held his hands out, asking in universal sign language for me to pick him up.

I did and settled him on my lap, remembering a time when my own son would sit exactly where Cody was now sitting.

God, it didn't seem like it, but that was over thirty years ago.

Jesus, how time flew.

"Never be afraid of asking out the best-looking girl in the room," I continued. "They may be stunners like your momma, but you'll never know if you have what it takes to persuade her to date you if you don't take that first step."

"I don't like girls. They're gross," Cody countered. "Did you know that the average female lifespan is longer than the male lifespan?"

I grinned. "Yes, I did know that one. Do you know why?"

"No, why?" Cody questioned.

"Because females don't do stupid stuff in their youth like males do. If they make it past their young adult years, they have a fairly even chance compared with females."

Winnie broke into our conversation. "What are you teaching my son?"

I grinned at the best-looking girl in the room—hell, in the whole fuckin' county.

"How to be a man."

Her smile was brilliant. "I'm glad that someone is teaching him those things. Isn't he a little young, though?"

I shook my head. "No. A man's got to start being a man young, because he'll be there before you know it. You've done a good job starting him with please and thank you."

Winnie winked, then blew us both a kiss before leaving again.

About ten minutes before, Winnie had walked over to ask me if I wanted to go on a walk.

I hadn't.

The next twenty-four hours I was off. I usually ran about four-to-five miles every day, and then lifted weights afterward. Tomorrow, I might consider running—or walking with her. However, after the day that I'd had, I wouldn't be walking or running or, hell, even eating healthy.

When I'd seen the crestfallen look on Winnie's face, I'd offered my babysitting services, and she'd accepted.

Which led to now, Cody dripping popsicle juices on my pants, and me checking out his mother in tight black pants that molded to her ass almost perfectly.

"Another," Cody ordered.

I tore my gaze away from his mother's ass and grinned. "You gonna eat that or just let it melt down your arm and onto my pants?"

"Melt," he said. "Did you know that the 'rule of thumb' is derived from an old English law that you couldn't beat your wife with anything wider than your thumb?"

I burst out laughing. "Where did you hear that?"

"Conleigh was watching a show that I was watching from the hallway. It said it there," he answered. "Did you beat your wife?"

I shook my head. "No. I didn't. Some men do, but that's illegal now."

"Good." Cody nodded surely. "I would've hated to find out that you did. Then you couldn't be with my mommy."

Before I could tell him that I would never do that to his mother, or any woman, he continued.

"My daddy kissed my mommy's best friend. And last week when I was over there, Morgan broke his arm. He was standing on the counter, trying to get the candy that my daddy had put on the top of the fridge to hide from the kids. He tried to jump from the counter to the fridge but missed. Daddy was with mommy's best friend outside drinking beer. Does beer taste good? Do you know if it was made in America?"

"The beer?" I questioned.

"No, the fridge," he said. "It's a Kenmore."

"I have no idea," I admitted. "I can Google it for you."

"Do that, would you?"

I grinned and pulled out my phone, then found out that Kenmore refrigerators were, indeed, made in the USA, which I relayed to him.

"What else?"

"What else what?" I wondered.

The boy jumped around like a jackrabbit.

"What else is made in the USA?"

"A lot of stuff," I said. "But a lot more of it is made outside of the country."

"I like stuff that's made in the USA. Only because it has our flag on it, though. Did you know that there are fifty stars on the flag?"

"Sure did," I told him.

"Did you know that five of the six flags planted on the moon are still standing?" He tilted around to look at me, gauging my reaction.

"Didn't know that, Cody," I admitted. "How do you find all of these facts?"

"I make Mommy read to me off of the Google," he answered.

"Mom reads him the headlines off of the current events every night, too." Conleigh came in, her laptop clutched in both hands. "And every once in a while, Mom will let him pick a random fact to read. Last night was the one about the flags."

That made sense.

"That's kind of cool," I said. "You want to hear a few more?"

Cody's eyes lit up like it was Christmas Eve, Christmas, Halloween, and Easter all rolled into one.

"Yes," he breathed. "Please."

His please was almost an afterthought, and I winked at him. "Good job."

Then I spent the next hour reading him random facts and having him point out his sight words as we did it.

I couldn't believe it, but I had a lot of fun.

And I also realized how badly I missed my own son being as young as Cody was.

The wonder in his eyes when he learned something new was just fantastic.

"Whatcha doin'?" I questioned Conleigh when I saw her smile light up her side of the room.

Conleigh's eyes flashed to mine. "Just talking to a friend online."

Something that put a smile like that on her face wasn't likely to be only a friend, but until she wanted to confide in me, I'd allow the parenting to stay in Winnie's court.

Conleigh was old enough now to make her own decisions in life. I just hoped that she wasn't doing anything stupid that would harm her for the rest of it.

***

Winnie

"I like what you said to him," I breathed, snuggling up to Steel as he scooted into the bed next to me.

I felt him grin as he placed a kiss on my shoulder.

I rolled farther into him and brought my mouth up to his bearded cheek and pressed my lips against those curly hairs that dominated the bottom half of his face.

"Did you mean to leave the back door unlocked?" he questioned, ignoring my words.

I rolled my eyes, and he squeezed my hip as if he knew I'd done so.

"Yes," I said. "I heard you coming and unlocked it. This new app is the bomb dot com"

He snorted.

"I like it myself," he said. "It's not the alarm company I would've personally chosen, but with that prick Anderson in town, anything is better than what you have."

I agreed.

The day that I got home from work—the day that Anderson had made himself known—I'd contacted a local alarm company. They hooked me up with not just an alarm, but also two outside cameras, one inside camera, two locks and a smoke detector system that contacted 911 if smoke was sensed. The whole set up was so cool—I could unlock the locks from my phone, wherever I might be.

It also had a passcode so I would never have to rely on a key ever again.

Cody and I loved it. Conleigh tolerated it.

As I was thinking about how much I loved my new alarm system, I felt Steel's hand slip down my backside, and then curl around to rest against the lips of my pussy.

He did this a lot, though, so at first, I wasn't really expecting this to go into anything more.

When Steel had surprised me at work after saying he most likely wouldn't make it for lunch, I'd eaten without any excitement for my food like I normally would have.

Then he'd pushed through the door, and I instantly became so freakin' happy I couldn't explain it.

Then he'd given me some of the best sex of my life.

"Got a call from my ex," he said into the darkness.

"Yeah?"

"Yeah," I felt him nod against me. "She has decided not to contest the divorce. As of five PM this afternoon, I'm no longer a married man."

I grinned and moved to hug him tighter when his middle finger breached the seam of my pussy and started to circle.

His finger dipped inside my entrance, causing my entire body to jolt.

"Always wet for me," he growled.

I couldn't argue with that. Simply laying in the same bed as this man was a turn-on.

We'd done this exact thing all of three times lately, but it'd been enough to make me realize that that would be a constant state for me.

It was as if my body simply waited him out, knowing that if I was patient, he'd give me what I needed.

"Please?" I whispered. "I don't want to be teased today."

He flipped us, causing me to shriek, and situated himself between my legs.

The covers were gone an instant later, and the next thing I knew, his beard was tickling the inside of my thighs. "Open for me."

His order made me smile.

"And if I don't?"

"If you don't?" he teased, biting the soft skin of my thigh. "Well, I'll have to just convince you."

And then he was running those smooth lips up and down my thigh, gently coaxing them open without saying a word.

Before I knew it, he'd settled his broad shoulders in between my thighs—thighs that I parted without having to be asked a second time. Then he was pressing a kiss to my bare pubic bone.

I'd forgone panties, knowing how he liked to have access to me— even though we'd only had a few nights like this together.

Most of the touches over the last few times we'd shared my bed were innocent. Today's, though? Most certainly not innocent.

"Steel," I whispered. "Why do you like to tease me so?"

Then I felt his tongue trail up the seam of my pussy.

I did a full body shiver. It started at my toes and ended up at the tips of my fingers.

His tongue was warm and hot, but the feeling of his breath against my wetness caused a shiver to follow the trail he'd forged.

"Sweet baby Jesus."

Matt hadn't been good at oral sex. Hell, Matt hadn't been all that good at anything. Sure, he'd had an impressive cock—nowhere near Steel's in size yet still a fairly decent sized penis—that was obviously big enough for my former best friend to want, but that he didn't quite know how to wield. Certainly not like Steel did.

My God…there were no words to describe his cock. Not and do it justice.

His arms moved under the backs of my thighs and curled around until his hands were resting on my lower belly.

"You know," he murmured, his hot breath brushing against the sensitive skin of my sex. "I watched you race once."

"Yeah?" I asked distractedly.

A lot of people had watched me race. I used to run in televised marathons, so it wasn't a stretch to imagine that he'd seen me.

"Yeah," he muttered. "The last one you did here right before you had your stroke."

He bent forward and nibbled lightly on my labia, causing me to jump.

"You were in those tight black shorts that were so short they could have been a freakin' bathing suit bottom," he continued, moving to the other side and following the same process all over again. "And the number that you had pinned to them? I think that was bigger than your ass."

I would've laughed had he not parted my labia with his thumbs and brought his mouth down to where I'd been needing him the most. But he didn't lick, he didn't suck—he only stared.

I doubted he could see as well as he usually could. The only light in my room at the moment was the street light shining into it— though that was fairly bright seeing as I'd been contemplating getting blackout curtains due to the amount of light that shined into my window while I tried to sleep. It was like sleeping during the daytime, sometimes. I'd even contemplated shooting it out with a BB gun, but seeing as there was a cop right next door, that probably wouldn't be a good idea.

With my luck, he'd catch me.

"And as I was watching you run in on that jumbo screen they'd set up, one of your strides lengthened, and there was this gap in your shorts."

I closed my eyes as I felt his breath flutter against my clit.

"And I saw your pussy…for just a little peek. A flash and it was gone…but it was enough. It was enough to set off a whole string of questions in my mind. Did shaving make you run faster? Did being bare drive you insane after twenty-six miles? Did anyone else see your pussy slip like I did?"

And then he moved the last half an inch, capturing my clit between his lips.

"Oh, oh sweet God." I nearly howled.

"Quiet," he growled. "You don't want to wake your kids, do you?"

No. No, I most certainly did not want to wake my kids.

I wanted him to fuck me.

I wanted him to suck my clit.

I wanted him to do everything to me. All at once.

He didn't do it all at once, but what he did do was enough to make me nearly lose my mind.

He tortured me by torturing my clit. Over and over he'd lick, suck and flick.

I was steadily squirming on the bed, and the only thing keeping me still was the steel banding of his arms that were wrapped around my upper thighs, holding me in place.

He tortured me for what felt like hours, bringing me to the brink of orgasm only to pull back and circle his tongue at my entrance—allowing my orgasm to wane.

He did this so many times that by the time I realized that he wasn't going to stop this time, I didn't have time to prepare.

The orgasm that overtook me was breathtaking. He tipped me over the edge with a flick and threw me so hard into an orgasm when he sucked my clit into his mouth that I screamed.

I couldn't help it.

Luckily, Steel was ready for it.

He withdrew one arm from around my leg and reached up my body just as my mouth opened in a scream. He muffled the sound with his hand as I orgasmed in his mouth.

His beard tickled my entrance, and I wanted him inside of me so badly in that moment that I couldn't help what I did next.

I was off my back and on top of him in a matter of moments. Before he could even react, I was sinking down on his extremely hard cock reverse cowgirl style, and he gripped my hips so firmly that it would likely cause bruises.

I didn't give one single fuck, though.

All I cared about was the way he filled me up.

The way he was hitting spots inside of me that no one else had ever come close to hitting.

I started to move, up and down. Then I swiveled left and right, causing him to groan.

"You gotta be quiet," I teased, breaths coming out in heaves. "We don't want to wake the kids."

He hissed something behind my back and urged me faster.

I complied.

I could feel my orgasm starting to build once again, and I knew that if we kept this pace, I would be coming. Not one single doubt in my mind.

And then I felt his thumb brush my back entrance, and the shock of it—something that wasn't wholly bad—caused me to squeal.

Oh, and come.

Let's not forget that part.

Apparently, my body liked the forbidden nature of the act, because I'd gone from getting there to being there in a few strokes.

"Steel," I sighed as the breath in my lungs fled.

He didn't brush that entrance again, but the knowledge that he had touched me there carried me through my orgasm. I came and came and came, and didn't ever want to see an end in sight.

Vaguely I was aware of him coming, too, but I didn't care.

I could only focus on me in that moment. The way he made me feel. The way my nipples were hard and peaked. The way my clit felt like it was on fire. The way my pussy was stretched almost to the point of pain around him. The way he reached so deep inside me that I couldn't tell from one stroke to the next whether it was pleasure or pain.

All of it was enough to keep me flying well past when his orgasm overtook him.

And when I finally did come down, literally straight on Steel's chest, causing him to grunt?

Yeah, I felt like my life had changed.

"I think," I breathed. "I think that we're going to have to do that again sometime."

He started to chuckle, then rolled me until I was on my side. He was snuggled up against me, still inside of me.

Neither one of us made a move.

Long minutes passed as our breathing went back to normal, but a nagging question kept fluttering around in my mind.

"What's gotten into you?" I whispered.

Not that I was upset or anything. I liked this frisky side of him. I liked being able to soothe his bad day away, even if it was with my body.

I'd talked to him after my walk, but he'd been pretty clammed up about what was bothering him.

Then, when I'd finally gotten him alone, his son had called.

He'd headed over to Sean's house because somehow Naomi had broken their kitchen sink and water was pouring into their kitchen and living room. Sean had turned the water off, but until they fixed it they couldn't use water. Hence Steel being gone for the majority of the night.

And also making me realize how much I'd come to rely on Steel's help throughout the day.

"I don't want to talk about my bad day. At least not all of it. There is one thing that we need to figure out." He sighed, long and loud, his hot breath hitting the skin of my neck as he did. "Did you get a call from your lawyer about Anderson?"

My belly tightened. "I did."

"And you heard?" he confirmed.

I nodded my head miserably. The hair of his chest tickled my lips as I did.

"We're not waiting for him to do something stupid," he promised. "We're going to figure this out. But, we're taking the right steps. Keep a log of when you see him. If he's within any length of space that makes you uncomfortable, call me. I'll come. We will have it on police record then."

I nodded again, not wanting to speak.

I could tell Steel was upset about it. Anyone with even a minuscule amount of brains could tell. And I had a feeling that, though this wasn't all that had happened today, it was one of the leading reasons he'd been so upset.

"It'll be okay," he promised, his large palm smoothing down my hair.

And for some strange reason, I knew it would be. The tightness in Steel's words made me realize that Steel had yet to let me down. And I knew he never would.

He was nothing like Matt. *Nothing.*

Where Matt hadn't told me a single word about Anderson being out of jail, Steel would go out of his way to make sure that I felt not a single ounce of fear. Even if we weren't together, I knew he would've been the first person to inform me that the man I'd put in jail was out.

I also knew that, if this ever ended, even badly, he'd never treat me wrong. He'd still spend time with Cody and Conleigh. He would never drop them like Matt had done.

When we passed each other on the road, he'd never curl his lip at me, acting like it'd been all my fault that we were over. No, Steel would stop. Talk. Make sure that I was okay.

And it would be pure, unfiltered torture.

Because I knew that I would never, ever recover from losing Steel. Not ever.

He was deep in my skin, and if the day ever came that he came to his senses and left, I'd be heading for a one-way trip to rock bottom.

I was in love with the man. I loved him. I loved Steel Cross.

I loved that he loved my kids. I loved that he loved his job. I loved that he dropped everything to go help his son. I loved that he asked how I was doing, even if it was in the middle of a movie or in a simple text. I loved that he sought me out to say hi if he came into the hospital. I loved that he brought me a cookie from a little old lady that had brought them to the police station for saving her cat. I loved that he was teaching my son how to be a man and my daughter how to funnel her anger into something productive. Even more, I loved how he wanted to make sure that all of his other officers were protected before him.

I just plain loved him and everything about him. There was nothing that I didn't love.

"Yeah?"

"Yeah, what?" I questioned, totally lost.

"Do you understand that this could get ugly?"

A little of my exhilaration fled.

"Yeah," I promised. "I do."

He pressed his lips to my forehead. "Go to bed."

I tried. I really did. But hours later, when I thought about something I wanted to add to my shopping list, I realized it was futile. But for now, I'd enjoy being in Steel's arms.

Here, there was nothing wrong. Here, everything was always right.

***

Conleigh

Sneaking out was surprisingly easy, considering the alarm.

I'd had to practice earlier in the day when I was the only one home, but eventually, I figured out that I had to hold my pillow over the panel on the wall and disarm it from the app on my phone. That way nobody heard that I'd deactivated it.

Really, the hardest part had been figuring out how to get outside without waking Steel. He'd come in only an hour before, and I'd semi freaked out that I wouldn't be able to do it. However, after turning off the alarm, I'd snuck out the kitchen window—which was the only window without the alarm due to the glass break sensor.

And as I ran to the car that waited at the end of the street for me, I felt exhilarated.

The closer I got to the car, the more excited I became.

Andy was in that car.

The car door opened, and my heart seemed to stall in my chest when I saw his beautiful smiling face.

He was older than I expected but no less beautiful.

My mom could date an older man, so why couldn't I?

Lani Lynn Vale

CHAPTER 17

Excuse the mess. My children are feral.
-Text from Winnie to Steel

Winnie

"And what's your chief complaint?" I asked the young girl.

The girl was cute. A blonde in her early twenties. Her face, though, had a tinge of green to it.

"I have pain," she whispered, then pointed down to her crotch. "Down there."

I didn't even blink at that.

Pain 'down there' was a pretty normal occurrence in the ER. This complaint was seen quite a bit and I wasn't sure anything could phase me anymore.

"When did this pain start?" I asked, standing up and walking around the desk.

"Ummmm, about four days ago. My boyfriend and I did some…things. It got pretty wild, but neither he nor I have been able to really remember what we did. I just know that next morning I woke up with my downstairs hurting and a killer hangover."

Oh, to be young again.

I nearly grinned as I tugged the blood pressure cuff off the wall and took her vitals.

"Have you been running any fever?" I questioned as I aired the cuff up.

"No?"

"You're unsure?"

She nodded. "I've been cold. More so than usual."

I took her blood pressure, wrote it down, and then reached for the thermometer.

101.8.

"You have nearly a 102 degree fever," I told her. "Fevers sometimes make you have chills. Especially one this high."

The girl nodded miserably.

"Okay, let's get you back there."

I gestured for her to follow me, and then walked her back to the only room available.

With the full moon around the corner, we'd had an influx of crazy patients today. Hopefully this girl would just be routine.

"All right," I pointed at the bed. "There's a gown here for you to change into. You can leave your bra on, but everything else has to come off. They will need a urine specimen. The cup is on the counter. Bring it back here to this room. Then have a seat and a nurse will be right with you."

I walked out and waved when I saw Sean pushing through the ambulance entrance, followed shortly by his much sexier father. God, the man did things to me.

An excited shiver rolled over me as our eyes connected, and I met him at the nurses' station with a smile on my face.

"Hey," I whispered.

He winked and then turned to talk to Dr. Tommy Tom who'd come up on his other side. I brushed my backside up against him as I let Ellen know that she had a patient.

"She's complaining of pain down below," I explained.

Ellen nodded, looking a little frazzled.

"Can you come in with me?" she asked. "All the other nurses are busy with other patients. You can start an IV for me once I get a look at what's going on…if it's needed, that is."

I nodded and turned to follow her, and felt Steel's hand brush my backside.

I grinned at him over my shoulder but kept going.

Once inside the room, I pulled the curtains open and smiled at the patient.

She was now in nothing but a gown just like I'd instructed.

She was shifting on her bottom, just like she'd done in the triage room, wincing every time she did.

Poor girl.

"Hi, my name is Ellen. I'm going to take a look at you today."

"Nice to meet you," the girl lied.

My lips twitched.

"All right, scoot to the edge and let's have a look," Ellen said.

Five minutes later, we were back at the nurses' station, Ellen standing next to Dr. Tommy.

"Uhhh," Ellen said. "Could you come look at something for me?"

Dr. Tommy's eyebrows rose. "Why?"

Ellen was completely competent and rarely asked Tommy for anything. This time, though...

"Ummm," Ellen just shook her head. "I just...I don't even know what's going on right now."

Tommy shrugged and gave Steel a look. Steel nodded at him. "I'll wait."

Tommy Tom and Ellen disappeared into the exam room.

"What's going on?"

I knew that he wasn't asking in general, but what was wrong enough to warrant Tommy Tom's help.

I shook my head.

"That woman has some things wrong downstairs," I finally settled on. "I've never seen anything like it."

Tommy Tom came out long moments later and gestured at me with his head.

I went.

"Can you go get me a suture kit, some saline flushes and a whole lot of gauze pads?"

I nodded and hurried to do what he asked, dropping them off to him a moment later.

Just when I was about to leave, though, Ellen said, "Please, stay. We may need assistance."

I didn't *want* to stay.

Not when I'd seen what I'd seen.

"Ummm," I hesitated.

Ellen gave me a look that said if I left, she was going to kill me after she was done.

I nearly laughed.

I stayed, but I stayed far enough back that I couldn't quite see what was being done.

Not until Dr. Tommy moved slightly, allowing me to see what was between the girl's legs.

Maggots.

Lots, and lots of maggots.

I nearly lost my lunch.

An hour later, I was white-faced, and walking out with Dr. Tommy and Ellen.

"That was…" I tried to find the words.

"That was a goddamn nightmare," Dr. Tommy muttered.

"What happened for it to get that way?" I asked hesitantly.

"Apparently, she thought that it'd be a grand idea to shove a piece of chicken up there for her unborn baby to have something to eat…"

I nearly vomited in my mouth.

"And it rotted?"

"And it rotted," he agreed.

"Gah, Dr. Tommy…" I did a full body shiver.

"Call me Tommy already. I feel like we should be forgoing the formal names, don't you?" he joked.

I shrugged.

Yes, and no.

Steel was the president of the motorcycle club, The Dixie
Wardens, or better known as the Dixie Warden Rejects around
these parts. Steel spent a lot of time with them, and Tommy was
right. I spent a lot of time with them, too. I probably should call
him by his actual name instead of adding the 'Dr.' in front of it.
But I couldn't do it. Not at work, anyway.

At least, that was what I'd found to be as of late. I'd tried, multiple
times, but I didn't want anyone at work that wasn't related to this
little group of ours to see me being treated any differently.

I already was semi-liked by all the other nurses and doctors.
Apparently, they didn't think that I needed special treatment
because of my stroke. I moved about 'perfectly fine' and I could
'do anything that the other techs did.'

Well, I couldn't.

I still got fatigued easily. I couldn't pick up a patient because my
legs just didn't have the strength to do it anymore, and honestly? I
didn't want to chance a relapse.

So, I didn't do everything the other techs did. Also meaning that I
didn't do the heavy lifting for the nurses and Dr. Stratton, AKA
Dr. Douchebag, that didn't like me.

Dr. Tommy had never treated me like that, nor had Ellen or Tally.

Yet, the other nurses, mainly the other charge nurse, didn't like
that she had to do extra work when I was on shift.

"I'll try," I lied.

Dr. Tommy—Tommy Tom—narrowed his eyes at me. "Why do I
get the feeling that you'll never call me that?"

"Because, *Dr. Tommy*," Tally said, coming up beside him. "She
doesn't want the staff to think you're giving her preferential
treatment because she's boning the president of your motorcycle
club."

I choked on my spit. "Really?" I choked out.

Tally blinked her eyes innocently. "Well, aren't you?"

I bit my lip and felt my face flush. "Well, yeah."

"Then, to be honest, you're going to get preferential treatment. Just like I do. Just like Naomi does when she comes in the door. All of the women that belong to a Dixie Warden are going to be treated differently by the guys in the club. That's how it should be, and how it always will be. We're in a league of our own, honey."

Was it bad that I really liked the idea of being in a league of my own with these women? Because I truly felt it in my soul when they all gathered around me whether it be at parties, here at work, or hell, even when I saw them randomly around town.

When Angelina and Matt had hurt me so badly, I never thought I'd have a friend again. Friending was too hard. The expectations that one had when friendship was involved literally scared me. But around the women of the Dixie Warden Rejects? Yeah, there were no expectations. Only friendship. No strings attached whatsoever.

And I also knew that none of them would ever do to me what Angelina did.

Then again, Steel would rather rip his own heart out than hurt me.

I knew that from the bottom of my soul.

Speaking of…

"When did Steel leave?"

"When are you going to call him Big Papa?" Dr. Tommy asked. "It sounds really weird when you call him Steel. I think there were only two people in this world that called him that, and both of them are dead."

My brows rose. "You're telling me I have to call him Big Papa?" I found myself grinning. "That'd be kind of funny, actually, when

225

we were going at it and I was like "Oh, Big Papa. Yes, Big Papa." I paused when Tommy Tom and Tally burst into laughter. "It's kind of like calling him daddy. I'll never be able to do it. Especially with our age gap. People would look at us weird."

"Not us," Tommy Tom wheezed.

"We could totally do the daddy thing if you wanted, but only in the privacy of our own bedroom," Steel's amused voice said from behind me.

I whirled around on the tip of one toe and gasped. "What are you doing here, Steel?"

My face was flaming. Again.

And Steel's amused face wasn't freakin' helping.

I started to back away, but he lurched forward and looped his arm around my hip, bringing me into his hard body.

I patted his chest and smiled, trying to play what I'd said off, but he wasn't going to let it go.

"Is that something that interests you?" he teased.

I shook my head forcefully. "No."

He grinned. "We'll see."

***

"Ride me, baby," he ordered five hours later, in the dead of night.

He'd come home so late that I'd already been asleep when he'd arrived—turning off the alarm and unlocking the door on his own this time.

I hadn't even felt him get into bed with me.

I had, however, felt his hands on my thighs and parting them.

I'd been partially awake when he'd swung me up over his hips and pushed himself inside of me.

And now, I was really, *really* awake as I rode him to completion.

"Fuck," he gasped. "Oh, fuck. Don't stop."

I tried, really I did, but the way he'd taken me over the last twenty minutes, despite me being on top, had taken everything out of me. Now all I was able to do was writhe on top of him while my orgasm took me over.

Before I'd come all the way down, he rolled, placing me on my back in the bed.

Then he started to take me with rough, hard thrusts.

"Oh, God," I mewled. "That feels so good."

His cock. The weight of his body pushing me farther into the bed. The breath stalling in my lungs.

Everything about it was so much of a turn on that one orgasm rolled into the next.

And just when I felt his body tense, I teasingly called him the name I'd been refraining from using in bed.

"Fill me up with your cum, Big Papa."

He did.

Oh boy, did he.

I'd have to remember to say that again to him the next time we did this very thing.

Lani Lynn Vale

CHAPTER 18

What starts with a P and ends with -orn?
-Popcorn
(You're such a perv.)

Steel

"So, will we be like…stepbrother and stepsister?"

I snorted as, Sean on one side, Conleigh on the other, sat glaring at each other.

"Conleigh," I tried to contain my laugh.

"You refused to let my mother work on your ambulance with you." Conleigh narrowed her eyes at Sean.

Sean didn't even blink.

"I refused to let your mother work with me because she can't lift a cot," he said, explaining why he'd denied Winnie a job.

I hadn't known that happened, and Winnie wasn't sore about it. Conleigh, apparently, was.

"You're a shithead," Conleigh retorted. "My mother doesn't need to lift the cot. That's what the EMT is there for if she needs help."

"Company protocol says she needs to be able to lift the cot. I don't make the rules, I just follow them," Sean shot back.

Conleigh lifted her lip in a silent snarl. "That's bullshit, and you know it. Ninety-nine percent of the time there's a volunteer firefighter or paid firefighter on the scene. I'm not stupid. You can't tell me that she'll only ever be alone lifting that cot. If, say, the EMT couldn't do it, there's always a family member there you could possibly ask for help. Or, hell, even a bystander of whatever scene you're on. It'd be a cold day in hell before there was no one there that could help. And my mom's getting stronger every day. She'd been PRN—part time as needed—since she moved here ten years ago. Then she had her accident, and you declared her unfit for duty. That extra two hundred dollars a month paid for my baby brother's clothes."

Sean's jaw firmed.

I'd bet my balls he hadn't known anything about Winnie when he denied her working there.

"He hadn't had a new pair of pants in a while until your father bought him some for his birthday last week." Conleigh rubbed salt into the wound.

And it *was* a wound.

I knew for a fact that Sean hadn't wanted to cut Winnie. He literally hated when someone couldn't pass, but he was right. There were rules set in place for everyone's safety, not just the patient's.

But, Conleigh was correct, too.

Ninety-nine percent of the time, a medic wasn't alone on scene. There was always a volunteer firefighter, paid firefighter, and sometimes even a cop on scene along with other random people—such as family or friends of the patient.

It was possible that she never would've been alone.

Sean, however, being an administrator, couldn't pass people because he wanted to pass them. There were rules. There always would be, and it sucked, but it was what it was.

"Okay, who wants pizza?"

Winnie's 'pizza' was homemade.

And, twenty minutes later, I found out that homemade pizza was better than ordering it.

"Holy shit, Winnie," I moaned as I took another bite of food. "This is amazing."

Winnie smiled.

"My parents used to own an Italian restaurant before my mom died. Dad got too sick to run it by himself…then I got pregnant right when I would've been able to help. He was so embarrassed by me that he refused to let me be anywhere near his restaurant—his pride and joy."

I don't think she'd meant to add that last part because she winced and looked at Conleigh.

Conleigh didn't look worried, though.

Thankfully.

The girl had a short trigger and lost it at the drop of a hat. Luckily this wasn't one of those times.

It was news to me, however, that Winnie still had a living parent.

I hadn't known anything about them, and Winnie rarely, if ever, spoke about them.

"Did you know that when a male honey bee mates with a female honey bee, the male ejaculates and then his penis explodes? Sometimes a queen can mate with up to fourteen other male honey bees. And she leaves a trail of broken wieners in her wake."

The table was silent until Sean said, "Interesting."

"Why would you want to mate when your penis exploded?" Cody asked the table in general.

Naomi started to snicker.

Winnie only shook her head.

"That's the million-dollar question, son," I told Cody. "And one we'll probably never know the answer to. Kind of like the praying mantis and the female ripping the head off when she's finished."

Cody blinked at me with wide eyes. "What?"

"Uhhh," I hesitated.

Was I not supposed to tell him stuff like this?

"When male and female praying mantis' mate, the female praying mantis rips the head off of the male's body when she's through," Winnie said without missing a beat. "Now, do you want pizza?"

Cody nodded. "Did you know that Americans consume over three billion pizzas a year?"

I just shook my head and stuffed another bite of pizza into my mouth.

Having my family all together like this was making my heart fucking happy.

"Dad," Sean said, interrupting my inner thoughts. "Did you ever think to share that you were the only freakin' person in the department that didn't have a ballistic vest?"

I blinked, then turned knowing eyes toward Winnie's direction. Winnie, who was avidly eating her pizza and looking anywhere but at me.

"I didn't think it was important," I answered.

"You just got my kid a freakin' jungle gym for her birthday that cost over a grand. That could've easily gone to your vest," he said, sounding annoyed.

"Yeah," I agreed, blowing a breath out in defeat. "But she wanted it."

"She also wants to have her fuckin' grandfather around when she graduates, or goes to prom, or gets goddamned married."

I sighed. "Sean, I'm not allowed to buy my own things for the department. It's company policy. Everything that I have has to come out of my allowance for uniforms, and seven hundred dollar vests aren't in my allowance."

The new bylaw was some bullshit rule that the city had come up with regarding new police procedures, and how police officers needed to be held to a higher standard or some bullshit.

I thought it was a fuckin' joke, but again, as the police chief, I couldn't very well buck all their policies, or they'd find a way to get rid of me—and my men needed me. They needed someone to look out for their best interests, something that hadn't been happening lately. Especially in this day and age where a police officer was no longer looked upon with respect but with derision.

My guys weren't bad. None of them, not even that stupid dumbass Matt.

Was he annoying? Yes. But he was good at what he did…well, you know, when he actually did his job and wasn't cheating on his wife.

"Well, we're going to fix that."

I grinned.

"I'm already working on it, son."

Just as I was about to have to explain how to my son, my phone rang.

Work.

"Hello?"

"Chief?"

I winced. "Yeah?"

It was Matt. Why the hell was he calling me on my day off?

"There's an incident at work. It has to do with Conleigh."

I looked over at where Conleigh was working on her third piece of pizza.

"What's going on?"

"I just think you better get down here."

I said I'd be there in ten minutes and then shoved my phone back in my pocket.

"I gotta go," I said. "Sean," I ruffled his hair, causing him to curse. "Naomi. I'll see y'all soon."

Before I left, I ruffled Cody's hair, just like I'd done to Sean, and received much the same reaction.

After passing Winnie and giving her a kiss, I left out the door chuckling.

I wasn't chuckling ten minutes later when I arrived at the station.

"What the fuck?" I asked.

Matt had his arms crossed over his chest, staring at the building and the cruisers that weren't currently being used by on-duty personnel.

"Who did this?" I asked.

"They're pulling the camera feed right now."

"You think she did this?" I asked.

"Her name is on the cruiser, Steel," Matt said. "And it's all over the school, too."

It was late. Well after ten in the evening. The nightshift was usually smaller, which meant that more than two-thirds of our cruisers were at the station.

Goddammit.

There went the money I was going to use on the remaining ballistic vests.

Mother. Fucker.

"She didn't do it," I said. "She's been with me all night."

Matt turned his gaze toward me. "Taking over my family?"

I laughed and then turned to fully face him. "I'm not taking over anything. I'm picking up the pieces. It's not my fault that you broke them."

"Cody is my son," he growled.

My brows rose. "You could've fooled me. What, you've only had him one week since I've been around, and, from what I've heard, you didn't have much to do with him that week. Conleigh told me that the majority of the time he was at your parents'." I paused. "You're lucky I didn't share that information with Winnie, or she would've been pissed."

Matt snorted. "Whatever."

I didn't reply to that.

"Yo," Tough said as he came up to us. "Kids. Multiples. But they're all wearing ski masks. No way to identify any of them except by the color of a few of the ones with long hair. Brown, red, and one with pink streaks in it."

"Conleigh has brown hair."

"Conleigh's name is on the cruisers, but she's not very popular at school thanks to you. I wouldn't put it past these teenagers to come here and do this because she has a job here," I said to Matt, then turned toward Tough. "Get what you can. Call that mobile cleaning crew we use when we have accidents, tell them we need our cruisers and station cleaned. Get the fire department to hook them up with the water situation. I want this cleaned up by morning. This will not get out."

"They'll want overtime," Tough offered.

I shrugged. "Then give it to them."

And, hours later, after reviewing the tape myself, I was sure that I could identify at least two of them.

One of them was wearing a pair of sneakers that I remembered seeing at a certain fight a few weeks ago. None other than Matt's new stepson, and the girl with the red hair that was his girlfriend.

I'd start with that in the morning, then go from there.

***

"Steel?"

I woke up instantly.

I'd been asleep an hour at most, but the moment Winnie said my name, I was wide awake.

After raising my son, then staying in this house with the woman I was falling fast and hard for and her kids—who I also cared about—I never slept deep.

"Yeah?"

It was still dark.

Really, really dark.

In fact, the only light that we had in the entire room came from the computer that Winnie had in her lap.

"I was thinking about something that I needed for Cody's Halloween costume, so I got on Conleigh's laptop because it was the first thing I saw. When I opened it, I saw this message on Facebook—the first thing that popped up when I opened the computer—and saw this."

I blinked the sleep from my eyes, and cleared my throat.

"What is 'this?'"

She turned the laptop around and showed me, causing my stomach to lurch.

"Who is that?" It was a picture of some guy's dick. "Some guy is sending her dick pics?"

She scrolled down more. "Keep looking."

The chat feed went on for what felt like hours. The beginning came about fifteen minutes later, and I finally realized that this all had started about two weeks prior.

"Andy. Did he send any other pictures other than his dick?" I asked.

Winnie shook her head. "No, nothing. His profile is bare, too. Just says his name is Andy Anderson."

The name Andy Anderson made my radar ping, and I was just about to come to an epiphany when Winnie interrupted my thoughts.

"*How to Lose a Guy in Ten Days*," Winnie suddenly blurted.

"What?"

"Andie Anderson is the heroine off of *How to Lose a Guy in Ten Days*," she repeated. "That's where I know that name from. It's one of my favorite movies. That's her. This guy spells his name differently, though."

My eyes flicked to the screen, and I slowly started to read over what was being said on the screen.

Andy: Hello. You're gorgeous.

Conleigh: Hi. Thanks.

Andy: You remind me of someone I used to know.

Conleigh: If you are from around here, it was probably my mother. We look exactly alike.

Andy: Haha, I don't know your mom. I'm only nineteen.

Conleigh: She works at the ER in town. Your profile says you're from Mooresville so you might've seen her there.

Andy: Maybe, I was in there last month for a cut that almost needed stitches.

My radar pinged again, but I continued reading, hoping it would come to me.

Andy: I'm okay. Just a minor cut. Didn't even need stitches.

Conleigh: I'm glad. Your profile picture is cute. I want a dog. When did you graduate from Mooresville?

Andy: Last year. Mid-year. I'm in college now. I'm going for my engineering degree. They make us attend bible classes here.

Conleigh: I'd fail. I haven't been to church since my grandmother took me when I was young.

Andy: You can always go with me. I could use all the help I can get.

Conleigh: Anytime. You never said you were on the football team!

Apparently, I was missing part of this conversation.

"Did you check to see if they were messaging on their timelines?"

"No," Winnie shook her head, the harsh white light off the computer screen lighting her face. "I haven't had a chance yet."

Normally, I wouldn't be so upset about this. But Conleigh was only sixteen, and this guy was nineteen and in college. Three year's age difference wouldn't be so bad if she was older, but she was so young, so the age difference here wasn't just a big deal, it was a huge deal.

Huge!

I read the entire length of the conversation between Conleigh and this boy, Andy, as it went from just talking about their daily lives to whether Conleigh had ever had an orgasm or not. The last entry was from last night at 11:59 PM.

Andy: Can't wait to see you again. Tomorrow. LY.

"LY," Winnie said. "Does LY think what I think it means?"

I felt sick to my stomach. "Love you, would be my best guess."

"So was this meeting for tonight or tomorrow night since it was almost twelve in the morning when he sent that last text?"

I got out of the bed and reached for my jeans that I'd discarded when I got into it.

"Only one way to find out," I admitted.

She scrambled up beside me and snatched the underwear that she'd left discarded next to the bed.

Then she followed me closely as we made our way through the house and down the length of the hallway toward Conleigh's room.

I moved to the side and gestured for Winnie to go in. "In case she wakes up."

Winnie snorted. "Her brother likes to come in her room at night. I highly doubt that she's going to do that."

Me, either, but it was always safer to be cautious.

I'd learned that after twenty plus years of being on a police force, and eight years of being in the Army.

Winnie pushed open the door and gasped.

"She's not here."

I followed her and felt my stomach drop.

"I'll put a BOLO on her," I muttered, taking one last long glance around the room before marching down the hall toward the bedroom and my phone.

"Did you know that there are thirty-two ways to fold a piece of paper and make it look like a dolphin?"

For the first time ever, I didn't stop to acknowledge Cody.

***

Two hours later, I sat on the arm of the couch and waited for Conleigh to finish sneaking her way in through the kitchen window.

Winnie was in the kitchen chair but scooted up against the wall of the kitchen right underneath the light switch. Her fingers were hovering over the switch, and she was glaring at Conleigh.

At least, that was what I assumed she was doing.

I wasn't glaring.

I was scared.

I was scared for Conleigh. I was worried that she was in over her head, and I was disappointed.

Disappointed that she'd done this when she knew it'd freak her mother out.

And, if I was being honest, I was hurt.

I was hurt that she was doing this when I'd gone out of my way to make sure she was safe. To make sure that she wasn't in trouble and had a job.

It was like she was spitting on my generosity.

Conleigh's flip-flops hit the floor, and Winnie finally hit the lights.

Conleigh gasped and turned, seeing first her mother, and then me farther beyond.

"Mom..."

"You're grounded."

Conleigh opened her mouth and said, "That's not fair!"

"You have a lot to learn." Winnie stood up, her feet a little sluggish, showing her growing tiredness. "And one of those lessons is this: you're grounded until I see fit to unground you. That means school, home, and work, if you have it, and then you come straight home. I'll be revising your admin capability on the alarm, and from what I heard when I signed up, I can give you a password input that'll tell me when you leave and when you arrive. So that means no more sneaking out in the middle of the night."

Conleigh looked flabbergasted.

I stayed where I was, not wanting to get into the middle of it.

I loved these two girls in front of me, but Winnie was her mother. I was just the boyfriend of her mother, not anything to Conleigh yet.

At least, I thought.

Then Winnie pointed at me.

"He had officers out looking for you. He used police resources. He WENT OUT HIMSELF. He was gone all night long, and I woke him up an hour into him sleeping to show him the crap I found on your computer—a computer that you will no longer have, by the way. He read it all right alongside me, and then immediately got into his car and started looking for you once we realized you were gone. He's more than gone out of his way to help you, and you've repaid his generosity by doing this?"

Conleigh looked at me like her favorite thing in the world had been stolen away from her, right out of her hands.

And I couldn't figure out if it was because Winnie had taken her computer away or had grounded her.

Then Conleigh surprised me.

"I'm sorry," she said, tears in her eyes. "I never meant to scare you."

I felt like the wind was knocked out of me.

"You should be. Because you just made one of the biggest mistakes of your life. Do you even know who this man is that you've snuck out to see?"

"His name is Andy."

"Andy Anderson doesn't exist," I said, breaking the silence. "I searched for him through the police database. No one named Andy Anderson, or anyone with the last name Anderson, graduated from the high school last year under that name. Or any other year, in fact. This man you're dating isn't who he says he is."

"You're...you're kidding." She swallowed

I shook my head.

"You could've been raped," Winnie said. "You could've been raped, then killed, and I never would've known you were gone until tomorrow morning when I tried to wake you up for school."

Conleigh's tears slipped free. "But Mom, I'm okay."

"Sure, right now," Winnie said, swiping away her own angry tears. "But who's to say that wouldn't have been a different story tomorrow? What if we hadn't found out today? This could've gone really badly, Conleigh. I can't even begin to count the ways."

"You don't know Andy."

"No," I agreed. "You're right. We don't, and that's the problem here. This boy, whoever he is, isn't who he says he is. Right now, we don't know what he looks like. His real name, or whether he's even nineteen like he says he is. Is he even from here?"

Conleigh looked torn.

"I…"

"Tell us," I urged. "This needs to be figured out. We need to know who this kid is, and we need to know more than what we've been able to pick up from searching his fake Facebook account."

"He's not nineteen. We never discussed how old he actually is, but nineteen isn't possible. He's, uhhh, maybe twenty-three or four."

"What kind of car does he drive?" I asked. "Did he tell you to call him by any other name? What does he look like? What color is his hair? Does he have any distinguishing tattoos? Do you know where he lives?"

She swallowed, then shook her head. "He's maybe five ten or eleven. He has dark black hair, brown eyes, and a small scar on his cheek. No tattoos that I've seen, either."

I looked over at Winnie.

Winnie looked ready to strangle Conleigh.

"Anything else?" I asked gently.

"N-no." She shook her head. "I've only seen him for about twenty minutes twice now. We've met down the block. He's always in a rental car. He said his is in the shop."

I nodded. "That's more than what I had an hour ago…time for you to head to your room."

Conleigh looked ready to argue, but her mother's snapped, "NOW!" made her hop to without a backward glance.

I looked over at Winnie. "Come here."

She shook her head.

I got up and went to her. Then wrapped her in my arms. "It'll be okay, baby."

"It will?" she asked. "Because from where I'm standing, I'm raising a criminal and a stupid child who could've gotten herself killed today."

"She's not stupid, baby," I soothed, rubbing my hand down her back and calming her shaking body. "She's a normal teenager who thinks, like we all thought, that she's smarter than we are. We all did stupid shit when we were kids."

She dropped her head to my chest.

"I hope you're right."

CHAPTER 19

In case you're confused, God would never send you someone else's
husband.
-Winnie to her ex-best-friend

Winnie

I watched, for the seventieth time in an hour, as the message chimed on Conleigh's phone.

Andy: You'll regret this, bitch.

Andy: I'll show you what happens when girls stand me up.

The messaging had started at 12:01 in the morning, and even now, at 12:36, they were still going strong.

"Just let him vent, baby," Steel murmured. "I'll be there in an hour. Just have to finish up a few searches. Love you."

I blinked and pulled the phone away from my face, staring at it like it was an alien life form I'd never seen before in my life.

"Love you?" I breathed.

LOVE YOU!

Did he really just say love you?

Oh my God!

I pressed the phone to my chest and tried to contain the freakin' smile that was threatening to break my face.

"Mommy, can I take this to bed with me?"

I looked at Cody, who was supposed to be asleep over an hour ago, yet was still going strong for some reason. It was like he was high on caffeine or something.

Though, I had a feeling it had more to do with the fact that I still had every single light on in the entire house. Or, quite possibly, it was because we were at Steel's place instead of our own.

We'd left our place around ten, and I was convinced that there was just something wrong with me. I didn't want to be in that house for some reason, so we came to Steel's place because I could breathe easier over here.

To say that I was nervous and scared was an understatement.

There was just something about this boy that was rubbing me the wrong way. Despite Steel's numerous searches, he couldn't find a single thing out about him, and it had us both concerned.

"Please, Mommy?"

Cody was wearing goggles and flippers—or mask and fins as Steel referred to them. I'd found out earlier in the day when Steel came by my place that tomorrow was the annual training for his SCUBA certifications. He'd had all of this stuff in his cruiser, but he had to take it out because apparently his vehicle had to be taken in for maintenance.

Cody, Conleigh, and I had helped him carry all of his stuff in. That was when Steel had discussed with both of my children—even Conleigh had listened entranced—what a certified scuba guy like him could do.

He'd showed them portable emergency oxygen tanks. He'd showed them his regulator, and answered Cody's eight million two hundred seven questions about SCUBA diving. The rest of the night, Cody kept sneaking in there to see the various pieces of equipment and then I'd help him research them online.

Before Steel knew it, Cody would be there in that water right along with him.

"Come on, buddy," I said and slammed the laptop closed. "Let's go put that up. Then it's time for bed. For real. We have a million and two things to do tomorrow, and I can't have you sleeping the day away."

"What are we doing?" he asked, walking like a penguin to try to keep the flippers on.

"Mom?"

I looked up to see Conleigh standing in the doorway of the room she was sharing with Cody for the night.

"Yeah?" I asked, still somewhat upset with her.

I say somewhat because I'd had a lot of time to think over the past several hours, and I was no longer as mad as I was when I'd first found her missing.

"There was a loud crash outside the window…did you hear it?"

I shook my head, then gestured with my hand. "Come in here. We'll take care of this heathen, then we'll investigate."

Conleigh followed, her steps mirroring mine as we waited for Cody to shuffle across the carpet toward Steel's spare bedroom where he kept all of his extra crap.

He also had a gun safe in there the size of a small Texas town, a spare bed, a freakin' motorcycle, and a toolbox that was nearly the same size as the gun safe.

To say the room was cluttered was an understatement.

I'd just bent down to help Cody get his flipper off when something akin to glass breaking followed by a whooshing sound caused me to jerk upright.

"What was that?"

"Come out, come out, wherever you are!"

More glass breaking.

"What the fuck?" I breathed.

I walked to the door and looked down the hallway into the house beyond it.

Steel's place was a lot like mine. It wasn't an open floor plan at all, but a bunch of defined rooms. So, it took me a little bit to realize that there was smoke in the air.

"Shit."

Another glass window broke, and I saw a bottle fly through the room.

It smashed against the wall opposite the window with a crash and that was when I saw the fire engulf the entire wall.

"Oh my God."

I pulled out my phone and dialed 911 as I moved back into the room, slamming the door and locking it.

"Conleigh! Get that comforter off the bed and shove it against the crack at the bottom of the door."

Conleigh started to move almost before I'd even finished instructing her.

Just as I was about to tell Cody what to do, the dispatcher picked up.

"911, what's your emergency?"

"My name is Winnie, and I'm at Chief of Police Steel Cross's house. There are...there are glass bottles with something flammable in them crashing through the windows. And the rags stuffed into the bottles are lit on fire so they ignite whatever's in the bottle as soon as the glass breaks. A man—I didn't see him, but he yelled something—was throwing them."

I couldn't remember what they were called but I knew that the dispatcher would figure out what it was.

"How many, and where are you?"

"I'm in the room at the end of the hall where his safe is located. Both of my children are with me. There are no windows in here, and the last bottle the man threw hit the wall right at the end of the hallway. There's not another room besides the bathroom for us to go to, and that window is too small for us to get through."

My voice sounded calm, but I was anything but.

I was literally shaking like a leaf, and the looks of fear on my babies' faces was enough to haunt me for the rest of my days.

"Units have been dispatched. Is there something you can shove against the door to keep out the smoke?"

"I've already done that," I answered the dispatcher.

"What about something wet you can wrap around your face?"

I didn't see a damn thing. Out of all the stuff in this room, none of it appeared to be anything that I could use.

Although, there sure was plenty of stuff that was flammable.

That's when I saw the first tendril of smoke filter through the vent in the ceiling and realized that this might not work out too well.

I looked at my babies, then took another look around the room, taking everything in. The gun safe. The motorcycle.

Steel's scuba gear.

Then I saw the portable tanks of oxygen, and I had an idea.

Placing the phone on the bed, I walked to the safe, entered the code—grateful to have a man like Steel who thought ahead and made sure I memorized his codes—and started pulling out guns by the handful.

CHAPTER 20

My favorite childhood memory is not paying bills.
-Sean to Steel

Steel

"Did they get out?" I breathed.

My house was standing, but it wasn't going to be fixed easily.

Water dripped from the ceilings and ran down the walls. Most of the windows were broken—either by whomever had thrown the Molotov fucking cocktails through my windows or by the fire department. I wasn't sure.

I had holes in my roof, and I didn't fucking care.

"We got Winnie out," one firefighter, Cook, said. "She was passed out next to the gun safe in your spare bedroom…but we couldn't find the kids. The Molotov cocktails were thrown in at the front three windows, one of which cut off the hallway from the rest of the house. It went up fast. Her call into dispatch said they were in that room. But she did make mention of a window in the bathroom. Our first thought was that they were able to get out there, but the glass is broken. No signs of anybody making it out of there. Winnie was bussed to the hospital about three minutes before you arrived."

I swallowed and stepped onto the first smoking cinder that used to be my front room.

"The kids," I croaked. "Have you searched for them at all yet?"

"That was our next step, Chief," Cook said faintly. "We have to move the walls on that part of the house, and for that to happen we have to wait for them to cool down."

I could see it. Everything had collapsed into itself. Really the only thing I could see standing in that part of the house was the floor-to-ceiling bookshelves that'd been on the wall of my office, but even those weren't in all that great of shape.

The rest of the house, though likely salvageable, was covered in water, soot and ash.

I headed to the part of the house where they'd found Winnie, no other reason than an instinct telling me to go there.

I looked around the area, covering my face with my shirt to avoid breathing in the soot and smoke that was still leeching into the room from the opposite side of the house.

I'd done this. I'd allowed this to happen.

That was why I was late today. That niggling feeling in the back of my head had finally shined bright in the forefront of my mind, and I'd connected the proverbial dots.

Andy Anderson was Anderson Munnick.

After acquiring a search warrant for his temporary residence—which had been at the low-income hotel in town, I'd gone with three other officers to either arrest Anderson or seize his computers.

If I could prove he'd done anything with Conleigh, I would have him. His being with a minor, while on parole for rape, would send him back forever.

I swallowed.

But he hadn't been there.

Why? Because he'd been *here*.

Terrorizing Winnie, Cody, and Conleigh.

I started walking through the house, ignoring the way my feet started to go through some of the walls that'd collapsed onto the floor.

If I didn't, my stomach started to crawl.

What was I stepping on? Could it be them?

I closed my eyes and tried not to think about Conleigh and Cody, or the way that they were probably buried under that pile of burning ash forty feet away from this room.

We made it to where they'd found Winnie when we came to a stop.

Everything in this room had been my pride and joy. At least, I realized it was until about a half an hour ago.

Then I realized that my prized possessions weren't things. They were people.

"The funny thing here is that she had all those guns laying around her. How many did you have?"

The question was asked so gently that I knew he was trying to broach the subject without tipping me over completely.

"We found her right there." Cook pointed to the spot next to where my guns lay in a discarded mess. "Do you think she was going to shoot the guy?"

"Maybe," I muttered. "I suppose it's possible if she felt that was the only way she could protect them."

A thump had me looking over at Cook, but Cook was just standing there with his arms crossed over his chest.

His bunker gear was half on, half off. His shirt was saturated with sweat, and his face was coated in grime. The only clean spots on his face were from the sweat that had poured down his cheeks and forehead.

"Did you say something?"

Thump-thump.

I turned back and looked at the pile of guns on the ground, and I immediately felt an almost irrational surge of emotion pouring through me before I catapulted myself toward the safe.

My fingers hit the safe's dial and slipped off as a layer of ash and soot fell away.

I wiped the entire thing off with my hand, then tried again.

43-99-36-96-12.

I'd never hated this combination more in my life.

I spun the dial and twisted the locks, swinging the door open.

"Stop touching me!" Cody shrieked.

"I'm not touching you, you're touching me!"

I'd never, not once in my life, been happier to hear two children fighting than I was in that moment.

I looked at the two children in the safe.

Conleigh had joked that it was so big she could fit in it earlier in the day…but I'd didn't really consider the idea of her actually fitting in there.

Apparently, she could fit in there, though, and so could Cody.

They had my two back-up SCUBA regulators in their hands, but neither was in their mouths.

And before I could process much more than that, two missiles hit me at my waist and knocked me backward.

"Steel!"

"Steel!"

As they cried in my arms, I felt sick to my stomach.

"Come on, you two," I said, standing up with both still in my arms. "Let's go get y'all checked out."

Conleigh was sobbing but managed to turn with me.

Cody hadn't even made it to the ground because he was clinging to my neck.

I turned, finding Fender standing on the concrete of my front porch.

"Did you check her feed?"

Fender nodded. "Anderson."

I closed my eyes with the confirmation.

"Fuck."

I started walking through the house.

Conleigh tripped at my side, but Fender caught her other arm and helped her along, but all the while neither kid let me go.

***

"I want him found," I ordered softly so as not to wake Winnie, who'd been admitted for the night for observation due to smoke inhalation.

They'd given her a few breathing treatments and started her on some antibiotics prophylactically, but otherwise, they'd given her a clean bill of health.

She'd passed out only moments before firefighters had found her. Having known the room that she was in, they'd come right to her.

The fire had been put out moments after she'd been pulled from the house, but it wasn't the fire that had been so destructive. It'd been the smoke.

"We've got every agency in the state looking for him," Fender said. "Called other chapters. They've got everyone looking on their ends, too. He'll be found."

I took a deep breath and then blew it out.

"Go home. Get some rest. Thank you for your help."

Fender smacked my back and then left without another word.

"You need anything?"

I looked over at Sean, who was standing next to the door.

He was working tonight, but he'd stopped in on his way out to make sure that Winnie was all right.

She was, thank God.

"No," I paused. "But Sean?"

He straightened himself up off the wall. "Yeah?"

"Don't let your guard down. This fool is all for Winnie and, by association, Conleigh. Don't let them out of your sight."

Sean nodded. "Truth and Ghost have the safe house locked down. Don't worry about them."

I laughed. "I wish it was that easy."

Sean left a few minutes later, and Winnie woke up, she broke my heart.

"I'm sorry."

"For what?" I asked, leaning down and pressing my lips against her cheek.

"For burning your house down."

"It wasn't you," I countered. "Don't worry your pretty little face about it."

She smiled. "It was Anderson."

The confirmation was good to hear, but I'd already known. "I know."

"I'm sorry."

And she kept saying she was sorry for the next ten minutes until her voice finally gave out. Even then, she kept saying it with her eyes.

"I love you," I promised her, causing her eyes to fill with tears. "Now stop worrying. The kids are safe. Every cop in the freakin' state of Alabama is looking for Anderson. Don't worry."

She closed her eyes, and then opened them again, indicating a 'yes.'

When she silently puckered her lips, I breathed a sigh of relief.

Too soon, it turned out.

***

Six hours later

My eyes snapped open as I heard the window break. Glass crashed to the ground.

I was at the safe house, along with Ghost and the kids, and trying to catch a few hours of shut eye before I started my own personal hunt for the douchebag who'd made our lives a living hell.

I'd been in the throes of deep sleep when the crash had woken me.

And then I heard the whoosh that only meant one single thing to me.

Fire.

I jackknifed out of bed and started running in the direction of Cody and Conleigh's frantic voices which were steadily rising in volume.

I found them in the bathroom that connected the bedroom that I was in with theirs.

My gun was still tucked securely in the waistband of my jeans, thank God, because I used the butt of it to knock out the glass.

Which was my mistake.

Because in doing so, I indicated to Anderson, who I now knew was outside, where we were. I yanked my face away from the broken window just in time, too.

I almost lost my face to a bullet seconds later.

"Fuck!" I hissed, backing away.

"Both of you out," I ordered, gesturing to the door.

Conleigh opened the door and moaned at the sight of the fire.

"I hate fire," she whispered just barely loud enough to be heard over the crackling flames that were quickly overtaking the curtains on the wall the bottle hit.

I agreed but didn't say it.

"Go," I ordered, pushing them both into the hallway before closing the door.

They went, and I pushed them around the fire, herding them into the room on the opposite side of the house.

It was the room that Ghost had been staying in, but when I pushed it open, there was no Ghost.

The window, however, was open and the curtains were flapping in the breeze.

A gunshot sounded again, echoing into the room, and I felt my stomach clench.

Then return fire sounded.

Ghost.

"Ghost!" I called out the open window.

"Present!"

I would've laughed had I not been so fucking scared.

Having two kids in a gunfight was definitely not something I wanted to experience ever again.

Add a fire to that gunfight? Well, let's just say I know exactly what my nightmares will consist of for the rest of my fucking life.

"Yo!"

Ghost came running out of the woods, and I blew out a breath. "Come on, you two."

Something cracked behind me, and I winced when I saw the door that had been closed was now open. A bullet had hit the door handle, and I highly doubted that it would be an easy repair thanks to half the door missing.

"Takes some balls to do it while *we're* here," Ghost, who'd come out of the woods like a wraith, said.

I handed over Cody, and Ghost took him with very little effort.

Conleigh crawled out moments later and then backed away.

The moment my foot hit the windowsill, something cracked behind me, and a sudden blaze of fire licked my right side.

And everything went black.

***

"Don't let her out of your sight." I heard my son's voice saying. "Take her out of state. Don't let her come back until this is taken care of."

I'd heard Winnie's voice at some point in this conversation, but the pain had sucked me back under before I could do or say anything.

***

Three days later

"I need y'all to do something for me," I said to the club that had gathered around my hospital bed.

"Anything." That came from Aaron.

"I need y'all to find this guy. I don't care how or if it's done legally. I just want to know that he's not out there, waiting around the corner to do this to them again. The law may not be on our side, but it's pretty damn obvious to me and everyone in this goddamn town that he did what he did because he wanted us dead." I drew a breath, and it burned. "I want you to find him. I want you to fucking rile him up. Then I want you to bring him here."

"What are you going to do once he's here?"

"Leave that to me."

Nobody argued, and I was thankful for that.

***

It took them less than eight hours to bring him to me.

He was roughed up, but he wasn't broken. Not yet, anyway.

"Anybody see you?"

Sean, my son, shook his head. "No, they didn't. We had a friend shut down the camera feed for about twenty minutes." His eyes missed nothing. "The staff on this floor is in the middle of a shift change. They won't be paying attention for at least another fifteen minutes or so…Dad, what are you going to do?"

I closed my eyes, then reopened them. "Don't worry about it."

Sean opened his mouth.

"Did you bring it?"

Sean nodded reluctantly. "Yeah."

"Let me have it." I patted the bed.

Sean walked around where Fender was holding Anderson steady and placed a bag holding my personal weapon on the bed.

Anderson's eyes went to it—the medium-sized black bag looked rather innocent.

I was sure there were also other things in there, but I was only interested in the one thing.

Sean, of course, didn't know what was in it. He only knew that it had a few things that I usually took with me when I stayed over at Winnie's place. Lucky for me it'd been in my truck for a little over a week now.

Otherwise it would have burned up in the fire right along with the rest of my shit.

I reached forward and tugged the bag up to me, ignoring the fact that my legs protested the action.

Then again, my whole body seemed to protest any action.

I had burns down the length of my chest along my right side that extended over the top of my right thigh and all the way down to my foot. I guess I should be thankful that it was somewhat localized to just one side instead of my entire body.

But the goddamn things still hurt.

"Let him go," I ordered.

Fender set him free.

"Y'all can go."

Sean hesitated. "Winnie…"

My gaze sharpened. "What about her?"

"She's leaving."

My jaw clenched.

She said she would.

I guess I shouldn't be surprised.

I'd heard from Sean earlier in the day that Winnie was refusing to stay with them. She wanted to be with me.

But I'd told them to hold her against her will if they had to. At least until we had Anderson in custody.

"I'll call her later," I said.

Sean just shook his head.

"This is not a good idea."

Then he turned and left, leaving me all alone with Anderson.

"Now's your one and only chance," I said. "Then I'm going to kill you."

"You can't kill me," he countered. "But this'll be fun."

It was.

For me.

Not so much for him.

CHAPTER 21

Dating older men doesn't make me sick. It does make me sore
sometimes, though.
-Winnie to her ex-husband

Winnie

"Mom, are you sure it's safe?" Conleigh asked.

I nodded. "Sean told me that Anderson is dead."

I didn't go into details about how Anderson had snuck into Steel's room at the hospital—or I'd been told. Or how he'd almost killed Steel. Instead, I stuck with only a partial truth.

Today, I'd realized two things.

One, I needed to leave Steel.

And two, I was almost responsible for not just my babies losing their lives, but Steel as well.

That was a very hard pill to swallow, and I was so done.

I was going to live my life by myself. I was going to raise my children.

What I was not going to do was move on with my life with Steel in it.

I couldn't do it to Steel.

Bad things happened to the people I loved.

I just couldn't chance it with Steel.

I'd have to do this on my own, and I wouldn't be putting anyone else's life in danger.

It made no freakin' sense, but it was my choice to make.

I just hoped it was the right one.

***

Steel

I hung up the phone and shook my head, a smile on my face for the first time in hours.

She thought she was saving me by leaving. She thought that she was cursed and that she would bring me bad luck if she continued to be with me.

That was what she'd said while I'd been half in/half out of sleep thanks to the pain meds they still continued to feed me.

When I'd woken hours before to her voicemail, I'd laughed.

Yes, she was confused. Yes, I knew she was gone.

No, she wouldn't stay gone forever.

Why? Because as soon as I was better and I could get out of this bed, I was going to walk out of this hospital and go find her.

It might be next week, or it could be three months from now. It didn't matter because I would make sure that she knew she was mine.

I would get her back.

And she'd never leave my arms again.

That I could guaran-goddamn-tee.

Lani Lynn Vale

CHAPTER 22

*If you say 'fuck it' before making a decision, it's probably not
something you'll be proud of.*
-Food for thought

Winnie

Four months later

It was my first 10K in over a year and a half. My first race since
I'd had my stroke.

My first race that I wasn't even remotely excited about.

After I had left Steel and moved out of state, I just didn't find
anything exciting anymore. Not when Conleigh passed all of her
classes with flying colors or when Cody finally mastered his sight
words. Not even when I lost six pounds or when I ran my first mile
without stopping.

Seriously, there was nothing inside of me that was even remotely
excited about this race.

The only thing that brought me here were a few friends who were
in the marathon scene.

This race was to benefit a scholarship in the name of a fallen
soldier named Dougie. They'd started this race ten years ago in his
memory, and all proceeds from it went into a scholarship fund in

memory of the man, who was also a parent, who had died while in combat.

Apparently, it was a big deal that I was coming back for my first race, and ESPN was covering my comeback.

And by attending this race, it would bring a lot of attention from the media to this great cause.

Which explained why I was there when I didn't run for anybody but myself lately.

"I'm so glad that you could make it."

I smiled at the two young women. Kayla, the one who'd started this race ten years ago when she was just thirteen, and her best friend, Janie.

I'd gotten a handwritten letter from Kayla begging me to attend. Since she'd gone to so much trouble to not only track me down but to also explain the race to me in a personal message, I'd agreed to attend.

Now, I was nervous as hell.

10K was pushing it for me right now, but I didn't want to let on that I was nervous about it.

I was leaps and bounds from where I had been a year ago, or hell, even just six months ago.

I never thought I'd be able to walk again, let alone run, but here I was.

I was back, and I was scared.

The gun sounded, and I nearly fell.

My hands hit the ground, and I looked up to see the entire stream of racers passing me by.

I got up and ran.

By mile five, my legs were jelly.

I hadn't felt my right foot since mile four, and my left thigh was screaming at me to quit.

But I wouldn't quit.

I wasn't in last place as I had feared I would be. Hell, I wasn't even in the middle of the pack.

I was fifteen to twenty people out from first place.

I knew I wouldn't win.

Hell, I knew that I wouldn't even get close to the man who was running the fastest—a male around my age named Raphael according to Janie.

He hadn't even broken a sweat, I didn't think.

He'd fallen back to talk to me a few times, checking to make sure that I was okay before he'd then hurry back into his previous position.

At first, it was nice.

Now, I was just angry that he could speed up and slow down as he'd done…multiple times.

Who the hell could run like that?

I knew that I couldn't.

Even when I was in peak shape, I couldn't just slow down and speed up. I had a rhythm, and if that rhythm was interrupted, bad things happened. Such as me not being able to make my legs work anymore.

Most of the people running this race weren't professionals. So it was understandable how he kept slipping back into first place just as easily as he held himself back.

But still.

Hell, I didn't even think I could be counted as a professional any longer. Not with being out of the running scene for a year and a half like I'd been.

But Raphael—Rafe as he'd instructed me to call him during one of his many pit stops to speak to me—shouldn't be able to do *that*.

Speaking of the devil, I watched as he crossed the finish line from about a half mile away.

We were on a long, downhill street—*thank God it wasn't uphill!*—that was the final stretch that led you to the finish line. I could see the runners in front of me, making it one by one across the finish line, as I ran.

The times flashed on the screen, one after the other, as each crossed.

Fourteen. Fifteen. Sixteen.

Seventeen. Eighteen. Nineteen.

Then there was me. Lucky number twenty.

I ran, no longer able to feel my entire right leg, and crossed with a fairly acceptable time.

Then I looked up and found *him* standing there.

Steel Cross.

Steel 'Big Papa' Cross.

My legs started to give out and I would've gone down hard, but he was there to scoop me up.

He wrapped his arms around me, and I could do nothing but wrap my arms back around him and hold on for dear life.

The entire four months that we'd spent separated hit me with the force of a battering ram, and I started to cry.

"You're here," I keened, burying my face into his neck.

My legs felt like limp, useless noodles as he held me, rocking me back and forth.

But he didn't let on that he was hurting.

Didn't act like he was in pain in any way, really.

Then again, I knew that he wasn't hurting anywhere near as much lately.

The burns on his chest and side had healed. That, I'd found out, from his son. His son that I called and checked in with once a week to see how his father was doing.

"Where else would I be?" he rumbled.

The sound of his voice was like a soothing balm to my very soul. Everything that had been rioting inside of me after the fires at Steel's house and then at the safe house where Steel was severely burned dissipated.

No longer was I scared. No longer was I weak.

Why? Because Steel was there.

He always would be.

I'd tried to stay away, and now I realized how stupid I had been.

It hadn't been until this very second, until Steel had reminded me how it felt to be in his arms when we didn't have doom hanging over our heads, that I realized what we'd been missing. What *I'd* been missing.

"I'm sorry," I breathed.

"Yeah," he rumbled. "We have some things to talk about, but right now, I'm just happy that you're here and with me. Happy that you finally made it through a race again. Happy that your son just told me eighteen useless facts while we waited for you to cross the finish line. Happy that your daughter was there to wrap her arms around me and tell me all about how her mama had ridden her ass for the last few months."

I choked on a sob and then squeezed him tighter.

"Did you see your time?" Steel asked a few moments later.

I licked my lips, then looked up to the giant screen that would tell me my time…and then gasped.

"Steel…" I breathed. "What did you do?"

"Nothing," he laughed.

I let go of him and stood on my own two shaky feet, and stared.

"Steel…" I murmured.

When I looked back at him, it was to find him down on one knee.

"Winnie?"

I couldn't breathe. Couldn't think. Couldn't decide whether I wanted to throw myself into his arms or let him finish with what he had to say.

"Yeah?" I croaked.

"We've had some good times, and we've had some *really* bad times," he started.

I dashed a tear away from my eye.

"Yeah," I agreed. "We have."

"And, over the last four months, I've done a whole lotta thinking."

"You have?" I asked.

Because I had, too.

I'd already decided I was going to go back. I was going to beg him.

I was going to do anything it took to get him to give me another chance.

He nodded, then pulled out a box that was in the front of his leather jacket.

The one I'd bought him for his birthday a few weeks before a fire that had destroyed everything.

"Yeah," he nodded. "And I know three things for sure."

I found myself smiling.

"And what are those?"

"One, I've missed the hell out of you the last four months." He grinned.

"Two?" I breathed.

"Two, I don't think I can live without you anymore."

I blinked back a tear.

"And three?"

"Three, I want you to marry me. I want you to hassle me about putting my socks away. I want you to yell at me because I forgot to put the tea up the night before. I want to lay next to you while you say sight words in your sleep." My lips twitched. "I want to watch you grow old. I want to sit at your side while we watch your daughter get married. I want to teach your son everything that I forgot to teach mine. I want you to be there when I take my last breath. I want you to never, ever leave me again. And to do that, I need you to say yes."

Before he'd even gotten the last syllable out, I threw myself into his arms while also screaming one word. Yes.

***

Hours later, we lay sated and breathless in the bed that I'd just bought.

It was a piece of crap from a surplus store, but it was a bed.

The kids had one identical to mine.

It'd been all I was willing to pay for at the time. Subconsciously, I think I knew that I was always going to go back to Mooresville. I knew that I wouldn't be staying in Kilgore long.

"Were you responsible for the three tactical vests that came to the office last month?" he questioned hours later, his breath tickling the skin at the back of my neck.

"Yes," I instantly replied. "But only for the one. The other two were matched by a local farmer's market. They thought it was a nice thing they could do. It was part of the proceeds of this race. We sponsored a few police officers in the state of our choosing. You were my chosen."

He started to snort.

"I'm glad I'm your chosen."

I was glad he was, too.

"Steel?" I asked after a while. "Did he really break into your hospital room?"

Something about what Sean had said had bothered me.

When I'd left that day, the black bag had been in our car that Sean had used to drive us to a safe house in Benton, Louisiana. We'd stayed with a fellow member of the Dixie Wardens, Loki, and his wife, Channing.

That bag, I specifically remembered grabbing a t-shirt out of before he'd left.

That bag had been with Sean.

Sean wouldn't have had a reason to be at the hospital after visiting hours if not to bring his father that bag. The bag that just so happened to have his backup revolver with it.

The bag that had magically appeared in Steel's hospital room with Sean nowhere in the vicinity.

"What you don't know won't hurt you."

"Steel…"

"No."

"Steel…"

He shut me up with his kiss. "No."

I didn't need his confirmation, though.

I knew that Sean, and maybe even the entire club, had brought Anderson to Steel. Then Steel had taken care of a problem he didn't see getting fixed any other way.

Steel Cross killed Anderson Munnick.

And I didn't care.

I highly doubted that I ever would, either.

Lani Lynn Vale

EPILOGUE

Your grandma has totally sucked a penis.
-You're welcome

Winnie

"Do you want any eggs?" Steel asked me, the island bar separating where he was standing cooking eggs, and I was sitting miserably at the bar counter.

"No," I declined miserably. "I don't want any eggs."

I ended that part on a snarl, and he looked down, but he couldn't quite keep the smile off of his lips.

He'd royally fucked up, and he knew it.

Hell, I knew it, too.

Stupid, stupid, stupid.

"Mom, why don't you want these lovely butt nuggets?" Cody asked, holding up the egg that showed the stamp on it. "They came from the farmer's market. I saw the chickens they came from. Did you know that when the chickens are too old to lay, they just eat them instead?"

I blinked. "Please, don't ever refer to eggs as butt nuggets again. And, no. I did not. How do you know?"

"I asked," he answered, causing my mouth to quirk.

"He asked, and then he asked how the farmer killed them. When the farmer told them he wrings their neck, Cody then asked if he could help him do it sometime. The farmer told him that it could be arranged, and now you have an appointment to take him to this man's house next weekend so Cody can help kill, pluck, and process chicken."

I looked over at Steel.

"You're kidding, right?"

Steel shook his head. "Nope."

He popped the 'p' in nope, making me want to maim him. "Why?"

Steel shrugged. "Well, you did say that you wanted to quench his thirst for knowledge. This is the quenching part of his thirst for knowledge."

"I meant it in a way where you would have to deal with that crap, not me," I said, crossing my arms. "I cannot believe you."

Steel chuckled and cracked another egg into the pan.

"Mom, I heard from Matt." Conleigh said.

"Yeah?" I asked. "What did he have to say?"

"He said that he'd like to stop by next week sometime and take Cody and I to a movie."

I'd believe that when I saw it.

Matt was still the resource officer at her school, so she saw him a whole lot more than Cody did. Not that Cody cared. At least not until Steel and I had moved in with each other. Now Cody was all about Steel.

Steel can shoot eight bullets in the bullseye. Steel can piss without hitting the toilet seat, so he said I had to learn how, too. Steel can eat an entire row of Oreo cookies. That's my new goal in life. Steel can do this, and Steel can do that.

Steel, Steel, Steel.

I fucking loved it.

Steel had become a large part of our life, and six weeks ago when we'd gotten married, he'd also become permanent.

I knew he'd asked Matt if he would give up rights to Cody, but Matt had refused. And since Steel couldn't adopt Cody without that, Conleigh wouldn't hear of Steel doing it with her, either.

Which left us a well-blended family.

Speaking of blended family…our doorbell rang, and without waiting for a knock, the door opened and closed.

Sean walked in moments later, and I looked up and smiled for the first time that morning.

His daughter, Molly, was in his arms.

"Molly!" I grinned, holding out my hands. "Come 'ere!"

Molly came, then threw her arms around my neck and squeezed with as much strength as her little arms could muster.

Sean grinned as he bypassed me for the skillet that was still sizzling.

Steel set my plate of toast down next to me, and I immediately picked up a piece and handed it to Molly.

Molly took it and steadily munched away as her father started cooking more eggs.

"Here, Molly Mine," Steel said, scraping an egg and a piece of bacon off of his plate onto another paper plate and passing it over.

I set her up on the stool next to mine and then reached for Steel's fork.

Steel rolled his eyes and got up for another fork. Once he had it, he reached forward and set it out on the counter next to his plate, then showed Sean something he'd found on his deer camera that morning.

After passing Molly her fork, I reached over for Steel's fork and took a bite of his eggs.

The constant nausea that was always present these days seemed to abate, and I frowned.

Testing another bite, I smiled when I knew that it was going to stay in there unlike everything else I tried to put in there. Then, before I even knew it, all the eggs on his plate—three in all—were now gone.

Sheepishly, I looked up to find Steel's incredulous eyes on mine.

"What?" I burped lightly.

He snorted and looked back at his son. "You can fry up four more, right?"

Sean was laughing silently at this point, and there was nothing I could do but shrug. "Sorry."

"It's okay," Sean said.

"Umm, no it's not," Conleigh piped in from behind us. "Daddy Steel…" She grinned at Sean who only rolled his eyes at Conleigh's use of 'Daddy Steel' and continued, "Asked mom if she wanted any eggs before this all started. When he went to turn the burner off, he asked once again if she wanted one. She again declined. Then she just ate all of his eggs and two pieces of his bacon. Bacon that we don't have much of since Mom made that baked potato soup last…"

"You made the soup without me, Mommy Winnie?"

I flipped Sean off.

Sean was thirty-four to my now thirty-three. It was odd and a little bit disconcerting that he called me Mommy Winnie, or mommy anything, but he and Conleigh thought it was hilarious. Since it was all innocent, I decided to let it slide.

"I saved you some." I pointed to the fridge. "It's in the container that Naomi brought over for me last week. Maybe we should just both buy the same Tupperware if we're always going to be handing it back and forth. That way when we trade it out it won't mismatch."

"But how will you know whose is whose?" Cody chimed in.

"Ummm," I hesitated. "We wouldn't. But if one starts running low, and the other has more than enough, we just take some back."

Cody nodded. "Sounds logical."

Sean and Steel burst out laughing.

I rolled my eyes again and asked Molly if she wanted any more toast. She did.

Which wasn't a surprise. That kid could eat like a freakin' horse, yet she was still skinny.

"Mommy, when you have your baby, I want to work as a trash man."

"What baby?" Sean suddenly asked, a frown forming on his face.

My face flushed.

"Why do you want to be a trash man, and why would you need to do that? Mom and Steel can afford their child," Conleigh spoke distractedly as she continued to do her homework—late as always. "You're ridiculous."

Cody and Conleigh had such adult conversations sometimes that it was downright scary. I remember at Cody's age, Conleigh was getting into my makeup and still cutting her hair.

However, I had a feeling that some of Cody's grown-up personality had a lot to do with Steel.

"Baby?"

"Told you that you wouldn't be able to keep that secret for long," Steel muttered, taking a seat at my side with a new plate of eggs.

I eyed those, too.

"Don't even think about it." He angled his body so that his back was slightly to me.

I pouted.

"Baby?" Again, Sean repeated himself.

"Yes, brother Sean. Baby. Do you know where babies come from?"

Sean rolled his eyes at Conleigh's sarcastic comment.

"Why yes, sister Conleigh. I do. You and Naomi will be sharing a pregnancy, then. I wonder if my child's niece or nephew will be born before or after him or her," Sean mused.

I burst out laughing. "Our luck, it'll be born after, and then we'll have yet another weird name going on between them like you two already do. I'm sure y'all won't let that opportunity pass."

And I didn't.

As much as Sean and Conleigh fought, they were actually quite fond of each other...like real siblings.

"I got a call today from an employer who wanted to know what kind of character I thought a 'Lizzibeth Cross' had. I told him that she would be a great fit for her company," Sean said, stunning me.

"You did?" I asked. "Why did you do that?"

Sean's grin was almost infectious. "Because this job was in Montana. Way the fuck away from here."

"Language, brother dear," Conleigh chirped.

Sean flipped her off.

"Children," Steel drawled, humor lacing his voice.

I grinned.

I loved the brother/sister dynamic those two had.

He'd also helped her with school quite a bit, too.

After Angelina's son and her son's girlfriend had been outed for trashing and spray painting the police station and seven police cruisers, they'd been sentenced to juvenile detention.

Once they were back, they started at an alternative school and were no longer going to the public high school with Conleigh. Meaning Conleigh's life got a whole lot easier.

Then again, so did mine.

Without having to worry about her day in and day out like I used to, I now had more time to focus on Cody. Cody, who was passing all of his classes with flying colors—and knew all of his sight words. *Boom!*

Again, that had a lot to do with Steel, too. Having two parents doing the parenting instead of one helped not just the parent, but the child as well.

It also meant that I didn't have to work as many hours and got to spend a whole lot more time with my family.

"So, who was that boy that I saw you with last night, Con?" Sean asked, a gleam in his eye.

I turned to look at Conleigh, but it was Steel's "WHAT BOY?" that had me shaking my head.

"Steel," Conleigh said warily. "It was just a boy."

"What kind of boy?"

Conleigh glared at Sean. "You know exactly who he is, loser."

I studied the ceiling as Sean, Conleigh, and Steel started arguing, so I cleaned up my own plate and took a small, teensy tiny bite of an egg, that turned into an entire egg, behind Steel's back.

"So who is it?" Steel asked as I scraped my plate into the trash and then rinsed it off.

"It's a boy."

"Not a boy. He has a beard. Boys might have mustaches, not full-grown beards."

And that's when I knew exactly who she was talking about. There was only one 'boy' that had a full grown freakin' beard that I knew of, and that was Jessie James' son, Linc. The college football player.

"You're seeing Linc?" Steel barked. "And don't act like you didn't know the 'kid's' name, Sean. You knew exactly who it was. Why wouldn't you tell me this yesterday?"

Sean grinned.

"Because I'm a grown ass adult, and I don't have to tell my father when I see my little sister canoodling with a bearded man who is three years older than her."

While Steel was otherwise occupied, I took my shot.

Steel sat down moments later, still somewhat angry, and reached for his fork only to stop short.

"Where's my other egg, Winnie?"

I waved and kept walking with Molly's hand in one hand, and Cody's in the other. "Okay, you two. Let's play Candy Land."

***

Two hours later, I was dropping Steel off at the airport where he would be riding in a helicopter looking for what he called 'pot fields.'

"Thank you, baby." He leaned over the console of my new Jeep Cherokee and gave me a kiss. "Pick me up around five if I don't call."

I winked. "Yes, sir."

"Shithead." He laughed and got out.

"Have a safe flight," I said to him, pushing my door open and standing up.

He looked at me like I was crazy. "I have no say in the matter. I'm just a bump on the log in the grand scheme of things."

I don't know what made me say it. Maybe it was the hormones that were coursing through my body thanks to what he'd done to me— putting his baby inside of me. Whatever, I didn't care. But I said it.

"Die then," I said with a shrug and started to get back into the car.

He caught me up around the middle before I could so much as drop a single inch.

"Now, that was rude," he chided, nipping me on the ear.

I giggled and turned in his arms, placing one chaste kiss on his lips.

"I can't believe you did this to me," I paused. "Again. I never wanted to be pregnant again. Cody and Conleigh were hell on my body. I can't even imagine what this one is going to do to me."

He grinned unrepentantly. "I don't know what you want me to say. I can't help that I have feelings for you."

I sighed. "I have feelings for you, too."

He winked, then patted the roof of my SUV. "Drive safe. Text me when you get home. And don't eat all the leftovers like you did yesterday."

I shrugged. "If it's in the fridge, it's fair game."

He shook his head. "If you say so, woman. If you say so."

"Oh," I teased. "I say so."

***

Seven hours later, I was in a food coma and laying on my back naked in bed.

Steel was just coming out of the shower, and he was staring at me like he'd never seen me before.

"Is that seriously a Subway sandwich?" he asked.

I shrugged. "What if it is?"

"I'd say that you don't need to be eating sandwiches in the bed that we share because I'm not very fond of crumbs." He dropped the towel.

My eyes zeroed in on his cock, and I licked my lips, suddenly hungry for something else. Something that I couldn't eat, but I sure could taste.

I patted the bed beside me. "Come lay down and let me rub your back."

Because back rubs always turned into other things, and he damn well knew it.

He bent over and picked up the towel, laying it on the end of the bed, before walking over to the edge and flopping down.

I bounced slightly and then rolled, moving until I was straddling his hips.

"I probably shouldn't have eaten the sandwich," I admitted. "But I'll work off those calories."

"You're gonna go running tomorrow?" he asked.

I shrugged. "Maybe. Maybe not. I'm not really sure yet. The doctor said as long as I was running before, I could safely continue to run. But you heard that."

"I did," he confirmed.

Steel had gone with me to the OB/GYN appointment.

But, that had only been because we were both scared.

I'd been experiencing lethargy, muscle aches, and headaches that were sending me to bed for hours and hours on end. I thought I was having a setback due to the stroke, and we'd both been worried.

After seeing multiple other doctors, and having them say I was perfectly healthy, it was suggested to go see my OB/GYN by Krisney.

Krisney who'd said that her husband had said that I sounded like I was pregnant when she explained my symptoms.

Thinking I was forever going to be a mom of two and was perfectly safe from pregnancy thanks to my IUD, I'd written off the idea.

However, the more that I thought about it, the more sense it made.

Steel coming with me had been more of a hand-holding type of thing than my actually needing him there. Yes, I was more than capable of going to my own doctor appointments, but I needed him there for moral support. Just in case something happened like the doctor telling me I was pregnant.

Which, turns out, I was.

I'd left there the day before thinking that I was one crazy mother fucker for doing this a third time with a man more than twenty years older than me, but I couldn't find fault in something that was made from the love that Steel and I shared.

"Babe?"

I started moving my hands again and got to work on the hard knot that I felt just above his left shoulder.

"I was thinking," I said softly. "If this baby is a girl, we could name her Liddie."

He hummed. "And if it's a boy?"

I smiled, remembering last night's story about his deceased best friend. His name had been Stone, and he'd been the president of the MC before Steel. He'd also been a fellow cop, as well as the chief of police. Both jobs that Steel now possessed.

He'd told me how Stone had been shot by a gang banger. He also told me, even before last night, that he missed his best friend.

Something that I saw every once in a while when his gaze would go distant and a faint smile would cross over his face.

"I was thinking that if it's a boy, we can name him Stone."

I found myself on my back, and Steel between my thighs, in a matter of moments.

"You're serious?" he asked.

I nodded, suddenly finding a smile on my face. "A hundred percent. Stone Cross is kind of cute, right?"

I swear to God, I'd never seen Steel cry. But his eyes got a little misty, and he looked away.

"Nothing would make me happier. *Nothing.*"

I smoothed my hand over Steel's face, down his beard, and cupped his neck on both sides.

"Then it's decided."

He nodded. "You've made me one of the happiest men in the world, Winnie."

My lip trembled. "When all that was happening to me with Matt...I didn't think happiness would be in the cards for me again. I didn't think that I would find something like that again. And I didn't find that same happiness again. Because this, what you and I share, isn't something that I ever had before with anyone. This is something totally different, new and pure. Sometimes, when I wake up in the morning by your side, I can't believe that this is my life."

He smoothed back my hair. "This *is* our life, baby. Better get used to it."

***

Steel

Eight months later

"Stone," I said to the headstone. "I'd like you to meet your namesake. Stone Connor Cross."

The little boy that had defied all odds. The little boy that'd come kicking and screaming into this world, his hand securely wrapped around the IUD that was supposed to prevent him from happening.

Stone Connor Cross, my two-day-old son, raised his tiny fist in the air and then brought it down lightly on the stone.

Then, a cloud blocked out the sun, and a beam of light shone down onto the headstone, darkening everything but one word: LOVE.

ABOUT THE AUTHOR

Lani Lynn Vale is married to the love of her life that she met in high school. She fell in love with him because he was wearing baseball pants. Ten years later they have three perfectly crazy children and a cat named Demon who likes to wake her up at ungodly times in the night. They live in the greatest state in the world, Texas. She writes contemporary and romantic suspense, and has a love for all things romance. You can find Lani in front of her computer writing away in her fictional characters' world...that is until her husband and kids demand sustenance in the form of food and drink.